NEIL LABUTE

autobahn

NEIL LABUTE is a critically acclaimed playwright, filmmaker, and fiction writer. His controversial works include the plays *bash: latterday plays*, *The Distance from Here*, *The Mercy Seat* (Faber, 2003), *Fat Pig* (Faber, 2004), and *This Is How It Goes* (Faber, 2005); the films *In the Company of Men* (Faber, 1997), *Your Friends and Neighbors* (Faber, 1998), *Nurse Betty*, and *Possession*; the play and film adaptation of *The Shape of Things* (Faber, 2001); and the short-story collection *Seconds of Pleasure*.

ALSO BY NEIL LABUTE AND

AVAILABLE FROM FABER

In the Company of Men

Your Friends and Neighbors

The Shape of Things

The Mercy Seat

Fat Pig

This Is How It Goes

autobahn

autobahn

A SHORT-PLAY CYCLE BY

Neil LaBute

FABER AND FABER, INC.

An affiliate of Farrar, Straus and Giroux

NEW YORK

FABER AND FABER, INC.
An affiliate of Farrar, Straus and Giroux
19 Union Square West, New York 10003

Distributed in Canada by Douglas & McIntyre Ltd.
Printed in the United States of America
First edition, 2005

"The Pleasures of Limitation" was originally published, in slightly different form, in *The Guardian* on March 3, 2004.

Library of Congress Cataloging-in-Publication Data
LaBute, Neil.
　　Autobahn : a short-play cycle / by Neil LaBute.— 1st ed.
　　　　p.　cm.
　　Contents: Funny—Bench seat—All apologies—Merge—Long division—Road trip—Autobahn.
　　ISBN-13: 978-0-571-21110-4
　　ISBN-10: 0-571-21110-0 (hc. : alk. paper)
　I. Title.

　PS3612.A28A96 2005
　813'.54—dc22

　　　　　　　　　　　　　　　　　　　　　　　　　　　2004047114

Designed by Gretchen Achilles

www.fsgbooks.com

10　9　8　7　6　5　4　3　2　1

FOR WALLACE SHAWN

They change their climate, not their soul,
who rush across the sea.

—HORACE

Everything in life is somewhere else,
and you get there in a car.

—E. B. WHITE

Contents

The Pleasures of Limitation

I'm not a car person. I figure if I mention that, right off the top, it'll help dispel any worries that this is going to be a piece about American ingenuity, the power of the Industrial Revolution, and the great open spaces of the United States. Don't worry yourselves, dear readers, this won't have much to do with that.

If anything, I'm completely the opposite. From a car person, that is. See, my father was a professional truck driver (and a part-time son of a bitch), so I've tried to do as much as possible to distance myself from the man and his behavior. I like cities and people and the arts and that kind of thing. However, I've written this collection of short plays that take place inside cars—under the umbrella title of *autobahn*—the majority of which were staged in New York with a terrific cast as a benefit for the Manhattan Class Company. Why? you ask. Well, because I can't seem to stop myself from writing. It's a happy curse. More specifically, why plays that all occur in automobiles? Because I love the infinite possibilities that a confined space offers the writer, director, performer, and audience (I'll explain this later). And more to the point, why should you care? Not a damn reason in the world.

And now is later, so I'd better explain. A theater company in Germany—Bochum, to be exact—recently staged a one-act play of mine along with two of my short stories. Both of these stories happened to be set inside cars, and when I finally saw a photograph from the production I was totally enthralled by the sight of a young woman and an older man sitting onstage in a makeshift Ford, with nothing but two seats and a steering wheel to guide the imagination. I suppose I never really thought of those stories as

vehicles for the stage—having first written them as prose pieces—
and seeing that photo somehow reinforced my love not just of
theatricality itself but of the power of limitations.

I'll elaborate. Working as I do in the twin worlds of film and
theater, it's easy to get lost in the excess of motion picture
production and forget how gloriously freeing it is to work on a
theatrical stage. When anything and everything—i.e., money—is at
your disposal, the need to be truly creative often takes a backseat.
Even as a viewer, I sometimes wonder why we've become such
sophisticated, needy filmgoers—willing to travel to distant worlds
and ancient lands but seemingly unable to keep from giggling if a
rear-screen projection is used when a character is "driving" a car.
Why is that? A movie, after all, is nothing but a series of still photos
run past our eyes at a speed that simulates movement—so why
demand such authenticity within the context of the piece itself?
Films are nothing but colorful, noisy lies that bring us undeniable
pleasure upon their viewing. That's fine, but why the hang-up with
wonderfully false moments like outdoor sets built on giant stages or
action scenes that are executed in front of a screen? And if we do
occasionally accept them, why do we limit our enjoyment of such
things to space operas or science fiction extravaganzas? Why can't
actors have a picnic or mow their lawns in obviously false settings
and not start a ripple of guffaws in the audience? Don't ask me.
Hitchcock didn't seem to mind, and his films don't exactly suck. Nor
did John Ford have any problem slipping in such obviously
manufactured moments in the middle of, say, *The Searchers*, his
ode to the West and good old-fashioned bigotry. Now, the
studios of yesterday knew it was cheaper to produce these
moments in-house than to go on location. After all, it's usually
about profits in the movies. Studio chiefs did, however, understand
one basic principle of show business that we would do well to
remind ourselves of from time to time—sell the moment and people

will lose themselves in the artifice. Maybe embrace it, even. But today, for the most part, we seem incapable of enjoying overt falsehood—even in Todd Haynes's beautiful ode to fifties-era Douglas Sirk pictures, *Far from Heaven*; the audience I saw it with chuckled whenever Julianne Moore "drove" through town against an obviously fake backdrop. The theater, though, was built and has flourished for centuries on that very keystone: artificiality.

One of the first bonds that a theatrical audience makes with a group of performers is the willing suspension of disbelief. This means, simply, that a viewer says to him- or herself that no matter what takes place on that stage, I'm going to accept it. This doesn't mean it'll be of quality or moving or anything else, but just that he or she allows that it is possible for two people sitting on chairs to be driving a car, lost on a deserted isle, or floating in space. And that pact is one of the most elemental and beautiful in all the arts. In fact, it's basic storytelling around the campfire come to life.

When *autobahn* was first staged—a reading, actually, with scripts in hand—relatively little was done to create an actual sense of movement or the road itself. There wasn't any time! There wasn't even really time to do all seven pieces—two more pieces, four more actors, many more scheduling headaches, no thank you. Instead, I whittled the plays down to five and created an evening from that. I also felt that without a proper production period, which would allow us to rehearse in costume with lighting cues, we were better off following the old acting credo: "Less is more." In the end, each of the five pieces was presented in front of an audience with just two hours' rehearsal. The actors wore their own clothing, chosen by themselves, as appropriate for their respective characters. (The only real limitation I put on them was that they follow my strict color scheme of black-white-gray.) This sort of seat-of-your-pants production engenders a blind panic that is itself a kind of freedom— and it was a pleasure to watch great people (cast, designers, crew) band together on a single day and create a theatrical event from scratch. That night, the actors were inside "cars" and driving down the "road" merely because we said so. And I promise you, the audience believed it. They believed it because inside the auditorium we made a pact with one another, and for ninety minutes we all hit the highway together. It didn't matter who was sitting up there— Philip Seymour Hoffman appeared without having a single line of dialogue!—the actors transported the rest of us using nothing but sheer will and the perfection of their craft. Across the board, Paul-Amanda-Philip-Kyra-Brian-Kieran-Chris-Peter-Kevin-Susan were breathtaking in their simplicity. Actors sitting onstage with nothing but a script, a rudimentary set, and minimal lighting, communing with the audience while pushing all the right buttons—that is a sight that I personally never tire of, no matter how many times I see it.

Maybe I wrote *autobahn* in part because sitting in a car was where I first remember understanding how drama worked. My mother and father certainly provided enough of that. And hidden in the spacious backseat of a late-model American sedan, I realized quickly how deep the chasm or intensely claustrophobic it was (depending on how things were going up front) inside your average family car. I can still get a pretty good silence going myself these days when I want to—of course I learned from the best. Hell, I can almost make it echo in there if somebody really pushes me hard. Cars, like most everything else, have been used as covert love nests, battlegrounds, or places of refuge in the past. So why shouldn't we appropriate these inherently dramatic spaces for the theater while we're at it?

Years ago Wallace Shawn wrote a terrific one-hander called *The Fever*, and in the author's note, he spoke of a desire to see his play performed in living rooms, in front of audiences of ten or twelve people. I feel the same way. Theater is anywhere you make it. I hope that with this print edition of *autobahn* actors take the text and memorize it, gather their friends in their own cars, and take off down the road, filling those intimate interiors with my words and their emotions. That would be a pleasure to behold.

In today's film industry, it is a shame but hardly surprising when a movie collapses under its own financial weight. Films "fall apart" all the time—over talent, schedules, all kinds of things. But mostly money issues. In fact, it happened to me recently. When I read a story now about that kind of thing taking place—yes, we do occasionally read in America, in short, concentrated bursts (especially if there are color photos included)—I can't help but hang my head in fraternal pain for the filmmaker(s). But, you know, when your art costs millions of dollars to produce, what can you expect? Now, to be sure, theater can be a costly venture as well—just ask any Broadway producer—but the old-fashioned "Hey, kids, let's put on a show!" spirit that attracts and keeps many theater artists going will never be snuffed out. I'm sure of that. In fact, the pleasure I get from setting up a couple of chairs on a bare stage and getting down to work with actors and an audience will never be bested. I promise you. Peter Brook, that clever old bastard, was right on the money about the joys of an empty space. You should try it sometime.

And for God's sake, dear readers, the next time you see Jimmy Stewart "driving" around San Francisco in pursuit of Kim Novak, or John Wayne up to his horse's ass in fake snow, don't laugh. Sit back and relish the simplicity. There is great pleasure to be had in a world of limits.

—NEIL LABUTE, 2004

autobahn

autobahn was originally produced as a staged reading of five one-acts in the order listed below by the MCC Theater (Robert LuPone and Bernard Telsey, artistic directors) at the Little Shubert Theater in New York on March 8, 2004. It was directed by Neil LaBute; sets were designed by Neil Patel, lights by James Vermeulen, and original music and sound by David Van Tieghem. The production stage manager was Stacy P. Hughes. The casts and plays were as follows:

bench seat
Amanda Peet
Paul Rudd

autobahn
Kyra Sedgwick
Philip Seymour Hoffman

road trip *
Kieran Culkin
Brian Dennehy

long division
Christopher Meloni
Peter Dinklage

merge
Kevin Bacon
Susan Sarandon

road trip was performed in a slightly altered version to accommodate a male passenger.

funny

A YOUNG WOMAN *sitting in the front seat of a car. An* OLDER WOMAN *seated next to her, driving.*

YOUNG WOMAN . . . it's all the same, you know? How it looks out there, along the highway. It is. That's funny. I mean, not funny-ha-ha but the other kind of funny. What would you call that? Funny-strange, I guess. Or odd. Funny-odd. It's just . . . I mean, I didn't expect that. That stuff would seem so . . . familiar. It is funny. To *me*, at least. (*Beat.*) So . . . how's Dad? Good, probably. I'll bet he's good. Dad is always good. He's a *good* dad. I'm surprised he didn't come, that he left all this up to you. That's kind of unlike him. Unusual, anyway. That he'd do that. Oh, wait . . . he's out of town, isn't he? Didn't you say something about that on the phone, can't remember now. I think you did. Said he wouldn't be able to make it—not that he called me, told me himself, that would be very, you know, "un-dad-like" of him, but—I guess I do recall that now. He's not home. Where'd he go again . . . Milwaukee? Is this a Milwaukee week? Yeah, guess it must be. Huh. I just don't get that, not at all . . . why he insists on driving himself up every other weekend, going up there to see Grandma and Grandpa. They don't care if he does, don't even really want him to, I can tell, times I've been up there with him. They sit there, on that floral couch of theirs, and just stare at you. Through you, really, that would actually be a more accurate description of it. Them staring *through* you. Maybe it's her cataracts or whatever, or that blood-thinning medicine he's on, but it's like you're there, they can sense someone's in the room, but they can't completely make them out. I mean, specifically. (*Beat.*) Or . . . they're just not very nice people. That could be it, too. They could just be crabby, old, mean people who don't give a shit about anybody, and just because they look frail and cute and all that stuff doesn't mean a thing. Because we age, right, we get older and all that, but it doesn't change who we are. Does it? No way. It doesn't . . . I mean, just because some guy, some Ku Klux Klan guy grows too aged to put a rope around some black kid's neck, that don't mean he doesn't want to. True? That's what I think, anyway. Just 'cause we can't doesn't mean we wouldn't like to . . .

The OLDER WOMAN *glances over at her daughter. The* YOUNG WOMAN *flashes her a serene smile.*

YOUNG WOMAN Obviously I had a little time on my hands up there to think about stuff . . . (*smiles*) Yep. Lots of time. It was an interesting place, a lot different than the last one. Really pretty cool, which I've been meaning to thank you both for, honestly. I even made up a little note—hand-painted and everything in my art class—that thanked you and Dad for getting me set up in such a nice facility. Never sent it, though. Sorry. Meant to, but, you know . . . didn't. But it was awesome. Their "campus." And the boys were cute, so you two really did a bang-up job. Thanks, Mom. (*Beat.*) I thought they had a good program, too, you know, maybe a little heavy on the "higher power" stuff, perhaps a bit too much of that nonsense, but overall, very good. Good staff, tasty food, I even liked the name. Twin Oaks. Quite pretty. Like a little bed and breakfast place or something, nestled there in a picturesque setting . . . although none of us, when we were walking around the grounds or on hikes and stuff . . . we didn't see any oaks. Not a one. (*Beat.*) Oh, you know what was funny, this one night? You'll like this—there was a movie on, in the rec room, this old black-and-white movie on the TV—and you know me, right? I usually run the other way when you and Dad are watching that crap, *Gone With the Wind* or whatever, I'm outta there—but I plop down for a second, just for a minute or so, to sneak a little popcorn, I've really got the munchies from all the restrictions they have me on and everything. Like no cigarettes— you didn't tell me that when you guys shipped me off there. Left that one out, didn't you? Whatever—anyway, this show is on, and as it's happening, we all notice, really quickly, that the movie's taking place at this roadside café called the same thing: Twin Oaks. Isn't that weird? Yeah. It all happens—well, mostly all—in and around this café-slash-home where this married lady and some drifter guy kill her husband. Basically for love. I mean, they end up taking his establishment and everything, getting his money, but mostly it's just for love. Isn't that cool? Mom? That we were watching it—my "peers" and I—at Twin Oaks and the story's meant to be going on at Twin Oaks. Although, obviously, a different Twin Oaks. (*Beat.*) Well, we all thought it was pretty funny . . . and after, we shared a smoke before bed. A *marijuana* smoke. I know that's probably hard for you to hear and everything, but I'm supposed to be more honest now. That's part of my sobriety thingie—to be candid.

The OLDER WOMAN *looks over at the* YOUNG WOMAN. *Silence.*

YOUNG WOMAN Yep. And anyhow, that was all before . . . before I got things together. I mean, in a place like that—you can get anything you want, or to do, you can do just about whatever you'd like, if you want it bad enough. And that night, I did. But I'm better now. Totally all better. Right? You believe that, don't you . . . Mom? I know Dad does. He told me, last family session he came to, he told me that. Looks me right in the eye, which for him is . . . (*points to her forehead*) . . . right about here. But he looks at me, and he smiles—maybe even tearing up a little bit—

and he says, he says in that one quiet voice of his, "Honey, I believe you. I do." Which was just so cool. I mean, like, *moving* almost. I was almost moved by that. I was. And now here I am . . . out and clean and feeling pretty great. So.

The YOUNG WOMAN *stops for a moment, considering.*

YOUNG WOMAN I just think . . . I dunno. I think maybe it could be really easy to fit back in at home, in a way. I know the twins are off at school now and all, so that'll be different, but, you know, I just imagine that it could be an easy fit for me to get myself into the groove. To register down at the community college next semester and maybe get a job even, my old job back, or that sort of deal . . . I could do that. Absolutely. I know that's what you're hoping, Dad told me last week, he said that you guys are really "pulling for me." He used that term, which just about kills me . . . "We're pulling for ya, sweetie." Which is not even something he ever says, that's Grandpa's phrase, and he knows I hate it, because it doesn't mean anything, not really, it has no meaning, but I guess the fact that he was there, still in his suit from work, and drove up to attend the meeting says something, so it's fine. It's okay that he uses it, but I just can't really buy into it. Not completely. Because, like, what're you guys saying by saying that? Huh? Seriously, Mom, what? (*Beat.*) See, you don't even know, do you? Nope. Not really . . .

They drive on in silence for a moment. The YOUNG WOMAN *looks out her side window.*

YOUNG WOMAN . . . No, I think the only way to prove to you guys that your money was well spent is to be honest, like they said. Do my best to become a more truthful person, to say what I feel. To mean what I say. Yeah. At least with one person . . . that's one of their ideas, that you start it small and be completely on the level, always, with one person. So, you know, no matter what else you do, you are always gonna be true to that chosen individual. They stand by it, the counselors up there, say that it's the best way to get yourself back on the road. And I picked you. Mom. Isn't that neat? Out of everybody, I picked you.

The OLDER WOMAN *glances at the* YOUNG WOMAN, *then back at the road.*

YOUNG WOMAN And so, that's why, well, I just need to be open with you here . . . here in the car where you can't run into the next room or slam the door in my face or throw yourself down on the bed and start crying, this is the place to be honest. Right? I think so . . . (*Beat.*) I'm gonna do everything in my power to use again. I know I am, I can feel it. I've done the time there, up there at Twin Oaks, and listened to all the lectures and sat through the groups and whatnot, and I'm telling you . . . I can't wait to get my hands on some shit. Whatever kind of shit anybody'll give me. That's what I want. And I'll do whatever that person asks, or whatever it costs for it. I will. (*Beat.*) I know that's not what you wanna hear, Mom, I'm sure that makes you sick and hate me and that kind of thing, but I did learn that at ol' Twin Oaks. To be honest. They impressed it upon us, most strongly, and I walked away believing it. I mean, I told them all that other stuff, too, all the crap they wanted to hear about me getting better and the like, but I do sort of believe this honesty thing. Just sitting here, as we were driving, it came over me. This desire to be truthful. So there it is. The truth. I know I'm gonna relapse. Can't wait to, really, so if that means you wanna turn around and drive me back, then I guess so be it . . .

The OLDER WOMAN *doesn't turn from watching the road, nor does she turn the car around. She just keeps driving.*

YOUNG WOMAN . . . figured that's what you'd do. Just get home, right? That's what people always think is best. Get home. "Everything'll be okay, if I can just make it back to the house." Good one, Mom. Do it, keep on driving—or "trucking," as they used to say when you were young, "Keep on trucking"—tell Dad, call those emergency numbers when we get back to our place. That'll fix it. You bet. I gotta tell you, though, due to this whole "honesty gig" that I'm doing here—that I'll probably lie my ass off to everybody else if you tell 'em about our little chat. I will . . . I'll say we got into a fight, that you're making things up, you know, my "greatest hits." I mean, let's be honest—who's gonna believe you, anyway? You who calls Dad at work, pulls him out of a staff meeting when the pool guys don't show up. Or . . . when that one post office dude, the delivery man, was trying to break in? 'Member that one? He made the mistake of opening the *screen door* and you had the police over in, like, ten seconds! Yeah, I think I'll take my chances . . . so, you decide. It's up to you . . . Mom.

They drive on in silence. The YOUNG WOMAN *lights up a smoke.*

YOUNG WOMAN I wish I knew what movie that was, that we were watching . . . I'd love to see what the beginning was like. Or the name of it, at least. I'm sure you guys would like it, you and Dad. (*Beat.*) After . . . when we finished smoking, all of us—there was maybe like six, altogether—we went back in and caught the end of it. The counselors were just wandering around, doing their charts and making sure people took their showers and all that, and the six of us kicked back and watched the last part. They got caught, of course. That man and the lady. They eventually turned on each other, and then somehow it was okay, in court, I mean— which we all cheered at, when somebody gets off in court—and then they got in a car wreck. Yeah, so the cops think that he did it, this guy, on purpose. For the money. So he ends up going to prison and getting executed for something he didn't do. Which is so, you know . . . funny. Not funny-ha-ha, but the other one. Strange. Or ironic. It was funny-ironic, that's what it was. We thought so, anyway. (*smiles*) You should've seen us there . . . stoned like we were and sitting around, watching this thing and laughing our asses off. We were, Mom . . . just laughing and laughing and laughing. Even when they sent us off to bed . . . up there in the dark, in the other bedrooms, I could still hear some of the other people going at it. Just giggling away, all by ourselves. We found it all so damn funny . . .

The YOUNG WOMAN *goes back to looking out the side window. The* OLDER WOMAN *continues to drive.*

bench seat

A GUY and a GIRL seated inside a parked car.

GUY . . . what?

GIRL Nothing.

GUY No, honestly . . . what's up?

GIRL I just . . . (*shrugs*) That's all I wanna know.

GUY What? That I'm . . . I'm . . .

GIRL That you're not just blowing me off here.

GUY I'm . . . hey, I'm not. No.

GIRL So, it's not about that, right? You're telling me flat out "no."

GUY Yeah. I mean, no, I'm not.

GIRL Which?

GUY I'm, you know, I'm not doing that.

GIRL Doing what?

GUY Obviously . . .

GIRL No . . .

GUY . . . blowing you off.

GIRL You're not.

GUY No. Not at all.

GIRL Okay, good. Thank you.

GUY Sure . . . I mean, you know . . .

GIRL Just 'cause that's why people come out here. Usually. *Up* here.

GUY They do?

GIRL Yeah. Well, either that or to make out . . . those two things, most times.

GUY Huh.

GIRL Yep.

GUY Cool . . . (*waits*) That's, like, kinda interesting. I didn't know that.

GIRL Well, that's the case. So . . .

She looks over, expectantly. Waits.

GUY What?

GIRL Do you wanna . . . ?

GUY Oh. Umm . . . sure, yes. Uh-huh. Let's make out some.

GIRL 'Kay.

They do. For a few minutes. They've done this before.

GUY That's nice.

GIRL Yeah. I like the way you kiss. You kiss well.

GUY Thanks. You too.

GIRL Really?

GUY Definitely.

GIRL Good, 'cause you never know . . .

GUY No, you don't.

GIRL I mean, unless somebody tells you or whatever.

GUY That's true.

GIRL Me, I always thought that . . .

GUY What?

GIRL Nothing.

GUY No, seriously . . . what?

GIRL I just . . . I dunno. I figured that my lips were maybe too thin.

GUY Really?

GIRL Yeah. Like, when I look at 'em or whatever . . . they seem
    sorta thin. On the thin side, anyways.

GUY Hmmm. I never thought that.

GIRL Yeah?

GUY Nope. They're . . . good. I think you have a good mouth. Lips.

GIRL Thanks.

GUY Sure.

GIRL You wanna kiss some more?

GUY Okay.

And they do again. More and more. Nothing fancy, but they are definitely going at it.

GIRL 'S that enough?

GUY Ahh, yeah. That's good.

GIRL Felt okay?

GUY Really okay . . . more than.

GIRL Yeah? How much more?

He smiles and holds up his hands, indicating.

GUY This much . . .

GIRL That's a lot.

GUY Well, that's how much it was. It was this much more than good.

GIRL Great.

GUY Hey, I never said great . . .

GIRL Shut up! (*punches him*) You're kinda funny . . .

GUY Not really. Not so much.

GIRL Stupid funny. That's what you are.

GUY Yep. (*smiles*) It's pretty up here, you know? Very nice spot. Tranquil.

GIRL True.

GUY But with the lights from town out there . . . (*points*) . . . so you still know where you are.

GIRL Yes. Unless you're breaking up with somebody.

GUY What's that mean?

GIRL Nothing. I'm just saying . . . it'd be different if a person was up here for a reason like that. Then it wouldn't seem so cozy . . .

GUY No, s'pose not.

GIRL It'd kinda suck then.

GUY Yeah. That would.

GIRL Not just here, though . . . that'd suck any place it happened.

GUY Mmmm-hmmm. That's probably why they say that . . .

GIRL What?

GUY You know, from the song.

GIRL No . . . what're you . . . ?

GUY "Breaking up is hard to do." That one?

GIRL Oh, right. Yeah. (*Beat.*) Is that the name of it, or is it just a line?

GUY Dunno. I think that's the name of the thing . . . pretty sure.

GIRL Right.

GUY But, I mean, it's also a line from it, too. One of the lyrics . . . (*He sings.*) "They say that . . . breaking up is . . . hard to do, now I know, I . . . "

GIRL I, umm, I know how it goes. I've heard it.

GUY Sorry. Sure.

GIRL Okay. (*Beat.*) So, which one do you think they mean it's harder for?

GUY Ahhh . . .

GIRL The breaker or the . . . you know . . . the one getting broken?

GUY "Breakee." I think that's what they actually call it. The "breakee."

GIRL Yeah, that one. Which do you think?

GUY Well . . . it's probably tough on both. Right? I'd figure, anyway.

GIRL S'pose.

GUY Yeah. It was a hit when my parents were going out . . . that record.

GIRL Really?

GUY I think so. They still listen to it sometimes.

GIRL They own it?

GUY Uh-huh. Well, not, like, the single or anything . . . but on one of those compilation jobs.

GIRL A what?

GUY You know . . . *Power Ballads*, or that type of deal. A collection.

GIRL Oh, right . . . with, like, a bunch of singers all on one album.

GUY Yeah. It's a tape, but . . . same idea.

GIRL Right. (*Beat.*) Neat.

She looks at him for a minute. A full minute. Then slides over across the bench seat toward him. He makes a slight shift away but holds his ground.

GUY Hey.

GIRL You okay?

GUY Yeah. Totally.

GIRL Is there . . . what?

GUY Nothing. Nope.

GIRL Do you need to say something or am I just . . . what's up?

GUY Not anything. Really. Not a thing. (*mock serious*) All is well . . .

GIRL 'Kay.

GUY It really, really is. I mean it.

GIRL All right. I'm just getting a vibe . . .

GUY What? What "vibe"? There's not any vibe thing that I'm doing . . .

GIRL None?

GUY At all.

GIRL Fine. It's just . . . maybe it's here. This place.

GUY You wanna go?

GIRL No, it's . . . whatever. No biggie.

GUY We can easily go. Give the word and we're gone.

GIRL It's cool. (*snuggles*) Hold me?

GUY Sure.

He puts an arm around her, even plays with her hair a little bit. She closes her eyes.

GIRL I bet that's it.

GUY What?

GIRL It's just being here. In this place where guys take girls to break up with 'em . . . That's probably what's bugging me.

GUY Hey, let's head out . . . come on.

GIRL Nah.

GUY Seriously, let's. No prob'.

GIRL No, I'm just saying . . .

GUY And anyway, I'm sure lots of girls bring guys up here, too.

GIRL Why?

GUY For, you know . . . like, the same sort of reason. To break up.

GIRL You think?

GUY Sure . . . I mean, if this is a place where people do that, then sure.

GIRL But more guys break up with girls than the other way around.

GUY What?

GIRL 'S true. I've read that.

GUY Where? Where do they have info like that printed up?

GIRL Magazines . . . in different issues.

GUY And they said that . . .

GIRL Yes. Guys do that more likely . . .

GUY You mean, "more often"?

GIRL What?

GUY You said "more likely," but I think you meant "often." They do it more often than girls.

GIRL No. More likely . . . Guys are "more likely" to do it.

GUY Oh, sorry, I misunderstood. I see.

GIRL Plus, they always wanna drive, too. Guys. So girls probably hardly ever come up here to do that . . . on their own free will.

GUY No, maybe you're right. Yeah. At least not *of* their own free will . . .

The GIRL *looks over at him again. Silence for a bit.*

GIRL Were you just correcting me?

GUY Hmmm? When?

GIRL Just now, there . . . with that "free will" thing.

GUY Ahh, no. I was just . . .

GIRL I said "on" and then you said . . .

GUY It's just . . . it's a different way of saying it.

GIRL You said "of" like it was all . . . right, but then why . . . ?

GUY We meant the same thing. Honestly. I wasn't trying to, please, no. It was just the way I learned it.

GIRL Fine.

GUY I mean it. 'Kay? I do. (*Beat.*) Hey, I would never do that.

GIRL We can't all go to college here, you know. Some people work.

GUY I know that. I work, too . . .

GIRL You know what I mean! A real job.

GUY Hey . . .

GIRL I mean with benefits. Full-time, not correcting papers and stuff.

GUY Oh. Well, that's what a teaching assistant does. Grade things.

GIRL And that's fine, it's great that they give you cash for that, but let's be honest . . .

GUY What?

GIRL It's not a job. With, like, some future to it.

GUY Well . . . I mean, yeah, it is. Sure it is. You're prepared to teach. To be a teacher. That's a future, isn't it?

GIRL Sorta.

GUY What do you mean . . . why "sorta"?

GIRL No, I guess it is. That's a job. Teaching. Sure. (*Beat.*) You just don't have one now . . .

GUY Yes, I do! It's a job, of course it is . . . I get a paycheck, have these regular hours . . . so, yeah, it's a . . .

GIRL No, you even told me . . . they don't call it that. It's a . . . a, ummm . . .

GUY What? "Assistantship"?

GIRL Yeah! That's it . . . "assistantship."

GUY Technically it's a "fellowship," but . . .

GIRL See? It's different.

GUY I'm a "teaching fellow." That's how it's listed in the catalogue.

GIRL So then you're a "fellow" and I work. And that's why you have more time to spend perfecting the way I speak . . . pointing it out, anyways.

GUY I really wasn't doing that! No, I wasn't . . .

GIRL Doesn't matter. We understand each other, right?

GUY I guess . . . yes.

GIRL I mean, you see what I was saying.

GUY I do.

GIRL Okay. (*Beat.*) Wanna kiss some more?

GUY Ummm . . .

GIRL We don't have to.

GUY No, it's just that . . . I can't leap back into it when we're . . .

GIRL What?

GUY You know.

GIRL What? Breaking up?

GUY No! Stop saying that. No, just that we're . . . arguing or whatever. So, I can't do that. Turn it off and on like some . . .

GIRL All right, fine. It's okay. (*She sits up and slides back across the bench seat, away from him.*) Anyhow, it's true.

GUY What is?

GIRL What I told you about girls. They don't come up here to do that. Not usually, at least.

GUY I see. (*Beat.*) But people do break up, I mean, whether it's here or back in town, in the West Indies . . . it does happen. And I think women do it as much as—or almost as much as—men probably do.

GIRL Huh. Maybe. (*Beat.*) You're sure going on about it a lot.

GUY Well, I was just . . .

GIRL I just mentioned it. That's all. This is a hot spot for it, so I was pointing that out.

GUY Right.

GIRL So, it sort of surprises me that we ended up here, that's all.

GUY I just heard about it, okay? Heard that it was a nice drive up here, so I thought we'd . . . you know . . .

GIRL I even got dumped here once, so . . .

GUY Oh. Really?

GIRL Yep. Like, 'bout two years ago.

GUY Sorry.

GIRL No big thing. I mean, it was at the time, it was plenty big then, but, you know . . . you get past it. Right?

GUY Sure. I guess . . .

GIRL I did. I mean, went a little nuts there for a while, freaked out or whatnot, but it passed. I'm fine about it now.

GUY Good. That's . . .

GIRL He was a college guy, too. Yep. In for a two-year graduate thing like yours and . . . Forget it. How boring! Sorry.

GUY No, please . . . go ahead if you . . .

GIRL It was just that he . . . you know, we were together for the
whole time, inseparable, really . . . and then come May of his
second year, like, maybe a week before finals . . . we're up here
and he's pulling the whole "different people" speech out of his
ass like it was Scripture or something, like no one had ever used
it or heard it before, and I should understand and let him go off
to do his poly sci thing as if we'd never spent two minutes
together . . . (*Beat.*) He brought me up here for a picnic and
then laid that one on me over some cherry cheesecake. I
don't even like Sara Lee, so fuck that, I walked home. Walked
my ass all the way back to my parents' house, which is a good
four miles from here, as you know. But, hey, that was my last
trip up here, so maybe that's why I'm just a teeny bit
cautious . . .

*She slumps down against the back of the seat, sullen. He clears his
throat, then slides slowly over to her.*

GUY Well, that's not me. I'm not that guy, or doing that, or . . . so,
I'm just not.
GIRL 'Kay.
GUY I heard it was a nice view. One of the guys in my Wednesday
seminar said that it was very, umm . . .
GIRL Well, it is. It is that, so long as you're just here for that. Or
maybe to make out.
GUY Uh-huh. 'S a good spot for that.
GIRL Want to?
GUY Ahhh, sure. Please, yes.

They start to kiss again, kind of getting into it. The GUY *reaches
down to touch her breast and she pulls away.*

GIRL I didn't say I wanted sex.

GUY What?

GIRL Why're you doing that?

GUY I was just . . .

GIRL Kidding. I mean, sorta.

GUY I don't . . . I'm lost now. Are you . . . ?

GIRL I was just pointing out . . . you sure were able to switch gears that time, huh?

GUY Well, I . . . yeah, but . . .

GIRL It's okay. No apologies . . . I just was thinking that maybe we only oughta kiss for now.

GUY All right, that's . . . sure . . .

GIRL The other stuff's kinda heavy. You know? Since I was really thinking that you were bringing me up here for something else.

GUY . . . something . . . ?

GIRL The breakup thing.

GUY Oh. Right . . . no. I wasn't. Promise.

GIRL No, I know, I know that now, but I'm saying . . . all the way up. On the way here I was sure that's what you were doing, so serious and all when you were driving, and I figured . . .

GUY It was winding, that's all. It's a very winding road.

GIRL I know. I can see that, but at the time—in that moment—I thought you were doing that. Getting ready to cast me off or something. Just like that other guy did. And in the same place, too!

GUY No, 'fraid not.

GIRL Good. 'Cause I think I'd totally lose it if that happened. Like a complete seizure or whatnot, right here on your bench seat.

The GUY *laughs, but it's pretty hollow. He slides back toward the driver's side a bit.*

GUY No, no . . . whatever you do, don't ruin the bench! (*laughs*) This is a classic, don't you know that?

GIRL Sure. You've only told me, like, one billion times.

GUY It is, though. Buick only made this model for three years.

GIRL Huh. Neat.

GUY Yeah, and with the back end like that, and the unique window shape. It's a real beauty.

GIRL Your dad gave it to you, right?

GUY Yeah. As I was heading off to here.

GIRL That's a nice gesture. A gift.

GUY Yeah, well, it was the only thing he ever gave me. Of use, anyway.

GIRL So, you guys're . . . ?

GUY Yep. We are that. The way boys and their dads get. (*Beat.*) Distant.

GIRL Sorry.

GUY Don't be. I got the car, and as far as I can see . . . it was the only bit of him that was worth a damn.

GIRL Huh.

GUY Anyway . . .

GIRL Yeah. Anyways . . . (*Beat.*) Good news is, we're not here for that—so you can break it off or anything. Isn't that right?

GUY Yes. Not at all.

GIRL Thank God. Sweet . . . (*She slides over and kisses him on the cheek. He tries to smile, but it comes out rehearsed, too forced.*) They are too thin, aren't they?

GUY What?

GIRL My lips. They are, I can just tell.

GUY No! Please, not at all. I was just, you know . . . thinking.

GIRL Oh. 'Bout us?

GUY In a way, yeah. Yes. It's about us. (*He looks at her for a long beat, then clears his throat. He fidgets a little, then catches her* *eye again.*) 'Cause I like you. I do. I liked you from that first time I saw you in the Ben & Jerry's.

GIRL Hmmm.

GUY I did. Completely.

GIRL Yeah . . . but probably 'cause I gave you all those extra toppings.

GUY Well, that didn't hurt!

GIRL Yeah, right! Figures.

GUY It didn't! (*laughs*) I even thought about dumping you when you quit that place, but . . . 'S a joke. (*He laughs again; she does, too, but something about it doesn't sit well with her. She stops quickly, looks at him.*) Seriously, though . . . I did think you were great and I'm so glad that we started going out . . . It's been, you know, like, totally nice. It has. (*Beat.*) But . . . So look, I was gonna say that, umm, we should . . . (*He plays with the steering wheel for a moment, then tries a different approach.*) Anyhow, I don't think that's always what's happening between couples, if you really look at it. When one of them says that, or proposes it. A, you know, split. Sometimes it's not that, it's not strictly a breakup or a severing of their . . . right? Sometimes it's just that they seem headed in different directions and they maybe . . . It's only a suggestion of a "breather." A slight period of time spent apart. A respite. I've heard that one used, too . . . "respite."

GIRL "Respite," huh? A "respite" . . . and how's that spelled?

GUY Ummm . . . r-e-s-p-i-t-e.

GIRL See, now this sounds exactly like what that other guy said to me . . . I'm sorry, but it does. New words, maybe, but the same ol' thing.

She looks pretty angry; he tries to remain strong but withers quickly. Decides to spin it back the other way.

bench seat

GUY No, look, not at all! I was just trying to say that . . . See, I'd like to talk about the future, that's all . . . what our future might be.

GIRL Oh.

GUY Like, if you see us having one of those. A future together, I mean.

GIRL Well, yeah, duh. Sure. (*Beat.*) Sure I do.

GUY Okay. Right. And would that be . . . what? Here, or . . . ?

GIRL Wherever. They have Wal-Marts all over, so I can transfer anywhere.

GUY Right. Of course.

GIRL I know engineers work in all parts of the world, so I'm willing to do whatever. You tell me.

GUY 'Kay. It's just that . . . you know . . . I think it's gonna be . . . well . . .

GIRL My parents'd be fine with it, too, so no problem there. I mean, they'd probably wonder why you couldn't just get a job around here, what with the Boeing plant nearby and all, but hey . . . they're not the end of the world.

GUY Sure. (*Beat.*) You mean "it." It's not the end of the world.

GIRL I don't really like it when you do that. Correct me.

GUY Sorry, I wasn't . . . I was only . . .

GIRL Just so you know. (*He nods and stops, trying to regroup. She slides slowly over to him, cuddles again.*) Whatever you want, that's what I'd like. However you wanna work things out is cool. (*laughs*) I was just so sure you were gonna let me have it, you know, tell me to take a hike or something, that I was really shaking. I was almost kinda mad on the way up, I don't know if you noticed or not . . .

GUY Ummm, a little, I guess, but . . .

GIRL Yeah, I was sorta steaming. I mean, you have to understand . . . this guy before you—I showed you his photo that one time, remember?—he really hurt me and I think I'm so hypersensitive to another incident like that one that I'm still jumpy, I am. Like, two years later. (*Beat.*) Afterward, and I don't mean just when I was walking back home, but for months after, I wanted to hurt him, I really did. I would follow him to class and send 'im shit, all this shit through the mail, little dead field mice and crap . . . I was so out of it! Yeah. I'd find out when he was going on dates and stuff—his roommate was this one wrestler who marginally liked me—and I'd show up at the restaurant or down over at the Cineplex and go to the same show . . . whatever. One time, this once, I waited in some bathroom stall at an Applebee's for, like, an hour. I screamed at this chick he took to his softball game. I mean, like, in her face! (*yells*) AAAAAAAHHHHHH!!! If you could've seen her . . . man, it was priceless. (*remembering now*) See, he ended up having to take some summer classes to finish up, so I really let him have it. Totally spooked him. He even called the cops once, but I was, like, so what? Fuck him. I just kept it up, but was very sly about it, too. Made it seem all totally random, from these different mail stations in other towns and stuff . . . they couldn't really do a thing about it. The police. (*Beat.*) I got his new e-mail address about five months ago—through one of those "Find Your Classmate!" deals out on the Internet—and I've sent him a few nasty ones. These, like . . . all these pictures of horses shitting in a woman's mouth and various acts of that nature . . . because, you know, that's basically what he did to me. Just outright . . . took a shit right on me and then probably laughed about it, too. All the way home. (*thinks*) How do you say it in the past, anyway? You know, like, past tense? When you've already shit on someone . . .

GUY Ummm . . . "shat," I think.

GIRL Really?

GUY Yeah. It's . . . I mean, I'm not so sure if it's the same for *horses*, but with people, yes. It's "shat."

GIRL Well . . . that's what he did. This Mr. Grad Student with a Trust Fund. He shat on me and sent me packing, and that is wrong. That is a bad, bad thing to do to someone, a someone who loves you, so I said to myself, I said, "Hey, little man, no! Uh-uh! I'm not through with you yet. Nope. And maybe not for a long time, either." (*Beat.*) So, see, that's what I was thinking about on the way up here. Sorry if I was being all weird.

GUY No, that's . . . no. Didn't notice.

GIRL Good. 'Kay, that's great. (*She settles into the crook of his arm. He is frozen, like a deer on the interstate.*) You wanna make out some more, or should we go drive . . . ?

GUY Umm . . . huh. Why don't we, maybe, sit for a bit? All right?

GIRL Sure. Fine.

GUY We could just sit here . . . and relax.

GIRL That's nice.

GUY Yeah. Let's stay . . . and relax.

The GIRL*'s eyes start to flutter and she closes them. He is wide awake.*

GIRL Tell me again.

GUY What?

GIRL How much . . .

GUY Huh?

GIRL . . . you know . . . how much more it was. More than good . . .

GUY Oh. (*indicates*) This much. It was this much more . . . this, this much.

The GIRL *drifts off. The* GUY *sits with his hands held wide, his eyes open, staring off into the night.*

all apologies

A MAN *and a* WOMAN *sit in a parked car. Traffic zooms past.*

MAN I know what you're thinking. Seriously, I do. It's so obvious.
You're being completely obvious about it and I'm not saying
that's bad—or wrong or whatever—I'm just calling you on it.
Saying, "Hey, I know what you're up to." I mean, I totally get it,
this attitude thing that you're handing me, and I'm trying to tell
you that it's not gonna work. Uh-uh. Not at all. (*They sit in silence
for a moment. The* MAN *lights a smoke, then starts in again.*)
Look, I know what I did was shitty—sorry about that, I'll try and
watch the language here because I realize that it bothers you,
started this whole business, really—but I do, though.
Understand, I mean. Maybe not us, or what it means to be part
of a mature relationship or whatnot, but I'm aware of my general
shortcomings. My capacity for asshole-ishness. Yeah, yeah, I
know that's not necessarily a word, but it conveys a bit of what
I'm trying to get across here. Some sense of this thing's
magnitude for me. I think what we've got, this bond, or—call it
what you want—it's pretty awesome. And I mean like how they
used to use that word, too, back in the ancient days when they
were trying to calculate the oceans or the heavens, that sort of
deal. Not like kids out there today, when every *fudge sundae* they
eat down at the Dairy Queen is "awesome." Teenagers've ruined
that word, mostly, but it's still what I think of when considering
us. We are "awesome." And that's not bullshit—or bull-whatever,
I don't know what the nonswearing version of that would be.
"Bullcrap," I guess. That's the only other one you ever hear, but
it's pretty lame as an alternative, I think. I mean, you know, when
you really *dwell* on it. Not that "crap" couldn't have some power,
like, the same power as "shit" does, if back in the olden times
they'd've just switched 'em around, gave "crap" a little more
respect or however that works. But they didn't. No. One is

all apologies

completely strong and awesome—sorry, damn, I didn't mean to use "awesome" again so soon, because I don't want it to take away from my feelings for us. And sorry about the "damn," too, no call for that. But you hear me, right, what I'm on about with this line of thinking? Words have all this command over us because we let them, because some dude in his room somewhere, maybe one of those monasteries or that style of arrangement, just thought it up and then goes around blabbing to everybody that he's got it all figured out. One particular animal or vegetable or the like—just pick an example if you don't care for this one—is henceforth gonna be called such-and-such. And then all his monk pals, well, they start in on calling it that and, presto, we got ourselves a word that we're stuck with for centuries to come, like it or not. I mean, if it was up to me, I might not've called a cat a "cat" or some turnip by that name. Right? And who says "love" was the correct idea to go with or that it had all the right shit—sorry, "crap"—to mean what that feeling is? It's beyond me. I just know that I wouldn't have minded a crack at a couple items myself. Naming 'em, that is. I'm fine with "car keys" or "strawberries," all kinds of stuff, but that doesn't mean I love 'em, either. Most words are just fine, nothing more. Adequate. I mean, I'm not nuts about "golf." What the hell does that mean? Was it some guy's name, or a place, or what? They've probably got one of those kinda books available—you know, like those astrology types that you like, up at the checkout counter—one of those that can tell you about the roots of stuff, their origins, but that's not my point. No. What I'm hoping to offer up here is a feeling that I care about us very much, but maybe I just can't find the right dictionary-type words to help me out. Maybe some *Jesuit* fellow dropped the ball a few hundred years ago—back before they even called it a "ball"—and now I'm the guy suffering because of it. (*The* MAN *stops to see if this is*

helping as he stubs out his cigarette butt. The WOMAN *says*
nothing.) See, I always figured I'm not romantic, I can't get in
touch with my emotions, all that TV talk-show junk, when maybe I
just haven't got enough nouns at my disposal. It's a distinct
possibility, that's all I'm saying. And now I could lose all I've
worked for, my home, children, even you—the lady in my life—all
because of some fucking friar back in *Sherwood Forest*! And
sorry about the f-word there, I know that one's a biggie with you,
but it gets me kinda riled up, to know that our marriage could be
hanging by some thread as simple as that. Not enough *words*.
The fact that nobody took the time from building those missions
or saving a bunch of savages in the Congo to really dream up a
set of useful phrases that could help me out here, well, that just
really gets me. It does, because I need a little assistance on this
one, something that says, "Hey, I'm sorry." I mean, I guess I
could just say that, "Sorry," right? Just say it and be done with it,
but it seems like a total cop-out to me. Still, if that's what you
want, if that's what it's gonna take to wash away all the running
around and drinking and putting my fist through your windshield
that time and me chasing you down at the mall and screaming at
you outside the Penney's store there, then I guess I'll just say it.
If you want me to. If that makes you feel so damn special—sorry,
but I'm getting a touch indignant about this—then I'll say it and
we can go get some dinner. Pick the kids up from school and
head over to Chili's or anywhere you want. That's fine. I did a bad
thing so I guess I deserve the rubbing my nose in it like I'm some
new Doberman puppy. Hit me with a newspaper, make sure I get
the point. Well, I do, I do get it, and I don't feel I need the little
"life lesson," okay? Not sitting here by the side of the road,
anyway, thank you very much. Sitting right here with our
neighbors driving by—you did just see the Freemans go past,
didn't you?—and my hands all waving in the air and crap. You

don't think they can see what's happening in here? Huh? Hey, they're not stupid. I mean, he may be out of work and she might be a goddamn bitch, but it doesn't make them dumb. She's a little slow, actually, but I'm sure he figured it out. Point being, can you just put the thing in drive and get us outta here, we'll talk about it tonight upstairs? (*Silence as he waits for an answer. Not a sound from her.*) Fine. That's fine, sit there, sit and look right through me until some guy from the Pella store comes by and plants a fucking *window* in the center of my forehead. I don't care. I don't. Shit! Fine, you win, okay? You win the damn prize and maybe that Dr. John Gray guy will forge you a medal over on Mars or whatever damn planet he's living on these days. I-was-wrong. Is that what you want to hear? Is it? 'Kay. It was bad of me to call you a "cunt," whether we were in the Albertson's or not. It's not a nice word, carries a lot of meaning with it—not that *I* assigned any to it, but that's neither here nor there. It's some monk's fault, really, that's what it is. Or maybe one of those damn nuns. But I'll be man enough to stand up and take the rap. It was not nice, what I did. What's the Oprah lingo you like so much? "Inappropriate." It was "inappropriate" of me to use that sorta language around you in public, and I understand that now. I really do. It was wrong. I'm sorry. Really very sorry. There, is that what you wanted me to say? Well, good, because I've said it now, so that makes it all better—I am sorry. Sorry about everything. I'm sorry and I love you. Honestly. Now can we please just *go*, for chrissakes? Please . . .

He sits back and waits for a gesture. Anything. She continues to stare at him.

merge

A MAN *and a* WOMAN *in an expensive car. He is driving. She wears sunglasses.*

WOMAN Turn here.

MAN All right . . . So, there were, what, two of them?

WOMAN Yes.

MAN You're sure, just two.

WOMAN I think two, maybe three. No, it was two. Definitely two.

MAN Definitely?

WOMAN Pretty definitely.

MAN Pretty or completely?

WOMAN Pretty completely definitely. Yes. Two.

MAN Two?

WOMAN *Two.* Watch the road, please.

MAN Two guys?

WOMAN What?

MAN I'm saying, it was two guys, or like a . . . ?

WOMAN Yes, men. They were all men . . .

MAN All?

WOMAN Yes. Of course.

MAN No, not of course. It didn't have to be just men. It could've been a mix, a combo of some kind. A boy and a man. Or two women, for that matter. Hell, I don't know. I wasn't there . . .

WOMAN I know, I know. But it wasn't. They were men, I'm sure. Mostly.

MAN "Mostly"? See, no, that sounds like a bunch of different people.

WOMAN No, it doesn't. I meant "mostly sure." I'm mostly sure they were men.

MAN Oh, okay . . .

WOMAN All of them. Grown men.

MAN Wait a minute, you just said "all" again. Before it was "two."

merge

Why's it suddenly "all" now? What's that supposed to mean? Is it two or not?

WOMAN Yes, it's two. Two men. I think.

MAN Come on!

WOMAN Well, it's hard to remember . . . I'm a little tired.

MAN "Two" is what you said, distinctly. A second ago. You said that, and now suddenly it's a group, it's this "all," which could be like forty or whatever.

WOMAN No, I didn't mean that. I meant "all" like in "two of them." That's "all," isn't it? I mean, if there's only two of them, then two *is* all.

MAN Yeah, but you don't usually use that word, not "all," if it's only two. Like in "two" of something.

WOMAN You don't?

MAN No, I wouldn't.

WOMAN Oh. Are you taking the freeway?

MAN Nah, it's jammed.

WOMAN All right.

MAN I mean . . . if you had two dogs, what would you say?

WOMAN What?

MAN You get two animals, okay, two puppies for Christmas, you'd say . . .

WOMAN My dogs . . .

MAN But if you were counting them, then what?

WOMAN I have two dogs . . . right?

MAN Exactly!

WOMAN But I could say, "all my dogs," I mean, if I wanted to.

MAN Yeah, but . . .

WOMAN I'm just saying, I might. I do, sometimes. With different things.

MAN Really?

WOMAN Sure. It's a choice.

you're, like, "No, no, come on, no, I can tell something's up, please, please, please, you have to tell me, I won't say a word, I just have to *know*." And now you're yelling . . .

MAN Okay, fine. Tell me. I'm silent.

WOMAN It was dark in the room, and then they came in. The "two" of them. They "both" came in. There, is that better?

MAN Yes, thank you.

WOMAN They came in and I don't honestly remember much else. I sort of blacked out not long after that.

MAN You blacked out?

WOMAN I did, yeah.

MAN "Blacked out," like passed out or like someone hit you, something like that? Don't tell me somebody smacked you . . .

WOMAN No, I don't think so, no.

MAN You just "blacked out"?

WOMAN Yes.

MAN In a darkened room, with all these guys in there?

WOMAN That's right . . . Oops, see, you did it now.

MAN What?

WOMAN You said it, too . . . "all these guys in there." You said "all" when you meant two.

MAN No, I didn't.

WOMAN Yes, uh-huh, you did. I heard you.

MAN No, I wasn't meaning "two," I said "all" because . . .

WOMAN Why?

MAN . . . because I was trying to trick you, probably.

WOMAN What do you mean?

MAN To see if you stumbled, if you weren't telling the truth and you'd trip up by telling me there were more than two. More guys than just the two.

WOMAN Why?

MAN I dunno. Maybe I don't totally believe this . . .

merge

WOMAN Why would I do that? Lie to you?

MAN Maybe because you don't want me to be scared or angry . . . or because you're scared, or whatever. Hell, I don't know!

WOMAN Don't yell!

MAN I'm not!! I mean, I am, but I'm not trying to . . . you're frustrating me.

WOMAN I'm just trying to tell you what happened. You don't have to fool me.

MAN I just . . . Okay, so you blacked out. You blacked out, fine, I can buy that.

WOMAN Thank you. I did.

MAN All right . . .

WOMAN And I don't really recall much else. Turn up there, it's one-way.

MAN You blacked out . . . but the room was already dark. Right? Didn't you say that?

WOMAN Yes . . .

MAN So, how do you know you fainted, then, if the place was already pitch-black?

WOMAN I didn't say "pitch."

MAN Dark, then . . . you said "dark."

WOMAN It was. Darkish.

MAN But how can you tell?

WOMAN You . . . you're just trying to confuse me now.

MAN No, I'm not, I promise I'm not. I just wanna understand. That's all.

WOMAN Well, it *felt* like blacking out. Okay? The room was dark, like I said, it was quite dim, anyway, no lamps on or anything. I'd only been back in it myself for a few moments, and the door swings open and they're in the entryway. Silhouetted in the light from the hallway and their features in deep shadow. Murk. I turn and see them, both or the two or all of them . . . whatever . . . and then I feel like I passed out. Like it all just went black.

MAN I see.

WOMAN You wanted to hear it and so there it is. How it happened.

MAN So you fainted, then?

WOMAN Probably. Most likely.

MAN You fainted. Fine. You were scared and so that makes sense. And then . . .

WOMAN What?

MAN That's what I'm saying, "What?" You woke up . . .

WOMAN Yes, obviously I woke up. I flew home, didn't I? I'm here in the car with you, of course I woke up.

MAN No, I'm retracing the events, the steps. Just after.

WOMAN Oh.

MAN I'm saying you saw them, these . . .

WOMAN Men.

MAN Right, these "men," and you saw them, the image of them there, and then you dropped off. I got that. But after, what happened after? What were the steps after you woke up?

WOMAN Ummm . . .

MAN They were gone.

WOMAN Yes, they were all gone.

MAN I wish you wouldn't do that.

WOMAN Fine . . . both. They were "both" gone.

MAN Thank you.

WOMAN And I'm on the floor, but . . .

MAN But what? What?

WOMAN . . . I'm undressed now.

MAN Jesus.

WOMAN Yes, I'm naked when I wake up, I'm sure of that. Nude. And I sort of wake slowly, in stages. Almost . . .

MAN What?

WOMAN . . . I don't know. Leisurely.

MAN You woke "leisurely"? After two guys break into your . . . ?

WOMAN I didn't say "break." I never said that.

MAN Well, of course they . . .

WOMAN No, I didn't say that. Not "break."

MAN Yeah, but . . . they had to break in. Right? . . . didn't they?

WOMAN I'm not sure. Maybe they did. I dunno.

MAN Wai, wai, wait. You're not sure or you know? Did they or didn't they?

WOMAN Ahhhh . . .

MAN Tell me they broke in. You weren't stupid enough to open the door for them, were you? Dammit, honey, how many times have I . . . ?

WOMAN No, I didn't, but I might've . . . you know . . .

MAN What?

WOMAN Left the door ajar. Or something. Careful, it's a yellow . . .

MAN Oh God . . . how does this thing end?! For heaven's sake, you're in a Howard Johnson's, not some Taj Mahal! You gotta lock the door!!

WOMAN You said *no* shouting! Stop!!

MAN Fine, hell, fine . . . I'm not shouting. See, I'm calm. I-am-completely-calm.

WOMAN Better.

MAN Good . . .

WOMAN That's better.

MAN So, whatever, you forget the chain thingie, it doesn't catch, you leave the damn latch wide open like you're Old MacDonald, fine. The guys arrive, you drop to the carpet. Hours pass. Hours?

WOMAN It was light out.

MAN When you woke?

WOMAN Yes.

MAN So, morning, then . . .

WOMAN Un-huh. Maybe closer to noon . . .

MAN You woke up at *noon*?

WOMAN Something like that. Maybe eleven-thirty. I was exhausted . . .

MAN Okay, right, I understand . . . but what's the "leisurely" bit? I don't get that.

WOMAN What's not to get?

MAN How "leisurely" are you?

WOMAN I woke up, stood there a minute, stretched, wandered around a bit . . . like that.

MAN I see.

WOMAN Almost like it never happened. Like some dream . . .

MAN But you're naked, correct? Without clothes. On the carpet when you wake. Is this not odd to you?

WOMAN Yes, it is . . . different, anyway.

MAN Then I'm asking, What's next? The steps you follow. Do you throw something on, a house robe, and call the concierge, the police, what?

WOMAN Ummm . . .

MAN It was dark, so you've got no description of the two guys, but . . .

WOMAN I think I ordered up some coffee.

MAN No, I mean before that. Right when you regained consciousness.

WOMAN Oh. I, ahh . . . lemme see, I . . . Yeah, I ordered the coffee.

MAN Coffee.

WOMAN Sanka.

MAN Oh. Okay. Sanka.

WOMAN Then I called you . . .

MAN Got it.

WOMAN You can just pass the Cadillac . . . they're looking at houses.

MAN Fine. I gotta tell ya, I'm totally lost here.

WOMAN We're running parallel with Broadhurst.

MAN I don't mean driving! Sorry, I'm not yelling, I just . . . You're at this convention, right, you get jumped by two guys in your own room, you black out for, like, *twelve* hours . . . and you come back to life in the morning, order up some room service, and then give me a jingle? Is that about right?

WOMAN Something like that . . .

MAN I see.

WOMAN I maybe had a bran muffin sent up, too.

MAN Got it. Right. One muffin.

WOMAN You're angry, aren't you?

MAN Me? No . . .

WOMAN You said I should just tell you, so I'm saying it . . .

MAN No, I wanna hear it, but it just doesn't even . . .

WOMAN It's the events as I best remember them.

MAN Then good.

WOMAN This is Williams, at the next stop.

MAN I know, I know . . . So, did they take anything, rob you, or were you injured in any way, can you at least tell me that? Did you find any marks, or feel any sort of . . . you know . . .

WOMAN I'm a little sore.

MAN Sore. You're sore?

WOMAN Yeah. That was Williams, right there.

MAN We'll go to Miller, then double back.

WOMAN Whatever you want. Williams is quicker.

MAN So . . . you mean, like, sore back, or legs . . . they bruised you in some way? What does that mean, "sore"?

WOMAN No . . . sore down there.

MAN "There"?

WOMAN You know . . .

MAN Not "there."

WOMAN Yes.

MAN Oh God . . .

WOMAN Yes.

MAN Which means . . .

WOMAN I dunno. I don't know. I'm sore, that's all.

MAN Like you've been . . .

WOMAN Yeah. Like I've been . . . doing that.

MAN And? *And* . . . have you been doing that? I mean, did
they . . . ?

WOMAN What, force me?

MAN Jesus . . . yes, I guess.

WOMAN No.

MAN Thank you, God. You're sure?

WOMAN Not one hundred percent, but yeah, I think so, no.

MAN Wai, wait . . . they didn't touch you or not?

WOMAN Touch, maybe.

MAN They . . .

WOMAN I said "maybe." I was blacked out, remember? They
might've touched me a little when I was down or something—my
clothes were definitely off—but I'm almost fully certain they didn't
do the other.

MAN "Almost" isn't, like, the most reassuring word right now.

WOMAN Well, they didn't. I don't think.

MAN You think.

WOMAN No, I *don't* think . . . It might just be sore from walking
around Exposition Hall, everything's so far there, you know . . . or
when I fell, maybe. Something. But not that.

MAN All right.

WOMAN We can scoot up Barker, if you want. Do we have milk?

MAN Yes, I . . . this is unbelievable!

merge

WOMAN You don't believe me now?

MAN No, I'm saying "it," the episode itself, that's unbelievable. Not you.

WOMAN Oh, I thought you meant me.

MAN No. You want me to stop at the 7-Eleven?

WOMAN Not if we have milk.

MAN We do.

WOMAN All right then. Fine. Look, I had to tell you . . . I did.

MAN No, it's . . .

WOMAN I mean, once we started I just wanted to get it all out. The whole thing. Purge myself of it, you know?

MAN Right.

WOMAN Put it behind us.

MAN Okay.

WOMAN So there . . . it's out and we can move on.

MAN Yep. At least until they call us.

WOMAN Who?

MAN The authorities. If they find out anything, you know, leads or whatever . . .

WOMAN Oh, them. I see. I thought you meant . . .

MAN What?

WOMAN Nothing. The men . . . I thought you were saying if *they* called us.

MAN You mean the two . . . ?

WOMAN Yes, I misunderstood. I thought you were implying that all of them might call or something.

MAN There's that "all" thing again.

WOMAN Forgive me. I mean "two." If the "two" of them were to call.

MAN Why would they do that?

WOMAN No, they wouldn't, I just . . .

MAN Who in hell would be stupid enough to . . .

WOMAN No one. This is a four-way stop. They're waiting for you . . .

MAN Sorry. I'm not . . . Did they take your purse or something, your ID? How would they contact us?

WOMAN They wouldn't. I don't imagine . . .

MAN You didn't . . . did you give them a card downstairs? In the lobby, I'm saying. One of your . . .

WOMAN I . . . may have. Yes.

MAN Oh God . . .

WOMAN It's possible . . . I should never drink.

MAN Drink? What do you mean, "drink"? You didn't . . . no . . .

WOMAN And it may not technically have been the lobby . . . I mean, per se.

MAN No?

WOMAN I guess it might be seen as more of a lobby-slash-lounge.

MAN Oh. "Lounge," huh? You went into the . . .

WOMAN I suppose "bar" would be more . . . correct . . . than "lounge." It was their bar.

MAN The bar. A hotel bar.

WOMAN I just shouldn't drink. That's the thing . . .

MAN I know that. I've told you that.

WOMAN Really, I shouldn't. Wine cooler, anything, just makes me . . .

MAN But you did. After everything we've been through, you did . . . didn't you?

WOMAN What, drink? Umm . . . yeah, yes, I did. Have one. Drink.

MAN You drank . . .

WOMAN Yes. You know, it's not easy with those long seminars, you don't know anyone . . .

MAN Honey . . .

WOMAN . . . you're tired, you try to blow off a little steam, just have one beer, and then . . .

MAN Just tell me . . .

WOMAN . . . you say "hi there" to someone, it's only "hi," a face

merge **53**

you've seen in a brainstorming session, no big deal, you think, they're from Kentucky or someplace, a JIM or TIM written in below HELLO! You get to feeling familiar, and out comes the old business card. You know? It's a reflex, that's all.

MAN Sweetheart . . .

WOMAN It's not a come-on, it's not. You don't even find them interesting, not really. Because they all have the same story in the end. Wife, three kids, want a divorce—they're almost separated, really, living in town during the week but waiting it out until the children are old enough to—you just listen to see if you can pick out the little flourishes they've added to the story, like a joke they heard somewhere and embellished a bit.

MAN So . . . the police aren't really looking for anybody, then? Is that what you're trying to tell me here? Honey?

WOMAN Ummm . . . I don't think so, no.

MAN Since you'd have to call them first, right? And you didn't do that, did you?

WOMAN Not specifically . . . no.

MAN I see. And that would be because . . .

WOMAN Their faces, in the hallway there, with the light behind them . . . it was dark.

MAN . . . that would be because you invited them upstairs. Maybe. You got drunk and you were talking to some guys—both or two or all—and you asked them up to your room. Up there to be with you . . .

WOMAN I did black out . . .

MAN Oh.

WOMAN I mean, at some point during . . .

MAN When they first came in, like you said, or . . . ?

WOMAN I don't know. Just at some point along the way.

MAN Huh.

WOMAN You know I shouldn't have liquor . . .

MAN Yes. I do know, yes.

WOMAN Right?

MAN Since college I've known that, yeah.

WOMAN We can jump on the freeway right up here. We're probably past the clog now.

MAN All right.

WOMAN If not, we can get back off at Meyer and cut across town.

MAN Fine. And so . . . I'm sorry, and so the soreness is from . . . from you . . .

WOMAN Yes. From that.

MAN I see.

WOMAN It's quite sore, actually.

MAN Hmm.

WOMAN Sorry. I didn't want to tell you. I didn't. But when you looked at me . . .

MAN I was just picking up your bag and I saw something. Sorry.

WOMAN I felt like I couldn't hide it.

MAN Something in your eyes there, even with the tinted lenses on, I caught a thing in your eyes as I scooped up the Samsonite. So I asked you.

WOMAN You did.

MAN I was scared, the way you looked at me . . . I said I wouldn't yell if you'd just tell me. Tell me about it.

WOMAN And I have.

MAN And now you have . . . yes. You have.

WOMAN Well . . . I'm glad we had this little talk, actually.

MAN Yeah?

WOMAN I am, yes. You can never hide a thing like that away, I mean, not really.

MAN No.

merge

WOMAN Better to just . . . I thought the story of them breaking in or whatever might be easier, ease you into it or something, but in the end, it's better to just . . . you know.

MAN Right. Sure.

WOMAN So now it's out there. We can deal with it, right?

MAN Absolutely.

WOMAN Good. And we can start fresh . . .

MAN Uh-huh.

WOMAN I mean, start again, from here. Clean the slate and . . . This lane ends in, like, a block or so.

MAN Honey?

WOMAN Careful.

MAN Honey . . . I know you probably don't want to . . . you might not like to . . .

WOMAN I'm a little tired, actually.

MAN . . . but I just need to know . . . this "all" thing, the way you kept flirting with that word and then jumping back to "both" or "two" . . .

WOMAN Yes.

MAN Was it two? Or, like, more?

WOMAN I'm really pooped. Can we . . . ?

MAN I just need to . . . It was just two guys, right? You got blitzed and these two guys followed you up to your . . . it wasn't like, you know, some kind of, I mean, not like that Navy thing or whatever, Tailhook. Right? It wasn't that, right?

WOMAN It was really dark.

MAN Right, but I'm saying, you didn't . . .

WOMAN Darkish, anyway.

MAN I can deal with this, I can. I just need some . . . You don't really mean "all" like in the actual "all," do you? Like more than two?

WOMAN I'm just gonna lay my head down for a minute, okay?

MAN Sweetie, just stick with me for a . . . I understand it was hard to tell me and all, and I kept pushing you, I know that, but . . . it was just those two, correct? Both of them, these Kentucky guys, right? You didn't invite up . . . no. You weren't up there with a bunch of, not like a *whole* group of . . . just tell me that. That's all I wanna hear. That you didn't have some line running out your door there, that's what I need to . . . Honey? Tell me. Tell me that and we can be . . . Sweetheart, please, I need to . . . You didn't, did you? No, you didn't. I know you wouldn't do that again. Right? You would not . . . Honey? Angel?

WOMAN This lane ends. You'll need to merge.

MAN Angel? Tell me. Just tell me that. Please.

WOMAN . . . you gotta merge . . .

MAN Please. I need to . . . please . . .

WOMAN . . . merge . . .

The MAN *drives on in silence, stealing glances over at the* WOMAN. *Her head rolls to one side; asleep.*

long division

Two MEN *sitting in a car, driving. The* MAN *at the wheel does most of the talking.*

MAN . . . I'd do it. Yeah, seriously, I would. If I were you, I mean. If I were, like, in *your* shoes, I would totally do it. *Totally.* Why not? I mean, what's it hurt to go over there and do a thing like that? Nothing, that's what. No-thing. It doesn't hurt anybody, and it's right, so you should do it. Yep. Go for it. If you don't, you're gonna hate yourself, hate the fact that you let it go, some unfinished business, and it's gonna eat at you, I promise it will. I mean, it's already bothering me, you can see that, right? It is tearing away at who I am and it's really not even my stuff. Or problem, or what have you. And yet it annoys me. It really does. And once I tell everybody, well, then you're really gonna feel bad! (*laughs*) I'm kidding, I'm joking with you, you know that, but still—the point of what I'm saying is truthful. This is not right. It is not a right and just thing that's happening to you at this moment, and you're gonna dislike yourself if you let it go at that. Hell, I'm starting to dislike you already! (*laughs*) No, I'm just bullshitting you, that's me playing, but there's an ounce of truth there, you know there is. And when a man sees the truth, or hears it—I don't remember exactly how that saying goes, but—he better take heed. That's what they say, used to, anyhow, that phrase exactly. "Take heed." It's a Greek term originally, or maybe a Roman one—but they stole most of their good shit from other people, so that hardly counts—it's an old proverb, anyway. That is my point. It's ancient, and therefore should be heeded. "Take heed" must be heeded. Right? If you don't, then I dunno, I can't really help you. I should probably just pull over and let you walk the rest of the way to her place, because I'm of no use to you. To the likes of you. You and your kind. Because if you're not a guy who knows when to take heed, well then, I'm not sure I've got any good business being associated with you . . . then I need to take some heed myself. Gather up my heed and get outta Dodge . . . That's meant to be funny, okay? Get it? Dodge, 'cause I'm driving a Dodge, so I said . . . forget it. I suppose it should be "you," right, to make that work, "get *you* outta Dodge," but somehow it didn't seem quite as comical. I dunno. (*Beat.*) Look, I'm just trying to lighten all this up, while still retaining some sense of the gravity of what I feel. What I'm saying, in no certain terms—is that right, or is it "uncertain"? I dunno—I'm trying to convey my total support. I'm behind you, man. Completely. You should go do this . . .

They drive on in silence for a moment. The MAN *at the wheel can't stand it any longer and begins again.*

MAN I mean, whatever, I can just drop you off at home if you want to. That's fine. There's always tomorrow, we can do it tomorrow if you want, 'cause I'm home at three-thirty on Mondays, so you choose. I just don't think you're gonna be feeling so perky come the morning if you let this sit. *Dwell* on it, that type of thing. I say, go over there—you run in, she already knows you're pissed off about it so it's not like a big conversation thing you have to do . . . you just go in, unhook the controllers—'cause those are hers, right?—you untwist a couple wires and you're outta there, five minutes tops. You don't even have to *engage*, you don't . . . and if he's there, her new "man" or whatever, you just look at him while you're doing it. Stare him right in the face as you're crouched down there and fiddling with it. I mean, if you're lucky, then she's put it up on a shelf or something, made it easier for you . . . being all hunched over like that, it'd be harder to keep an eye on him. Still, do what you gotta do. That is your game system, man, you bought it, I was with you when you did, and I would stand up in front of Judge Judy or whomever and go to bat for you on that point. So, you know, it's your move. I'm either turning up here on Division or not. You have to be the one to guide me. (*Beat.*) And I don't feel like I'm being responsible here—I mean "irresponsible," that's the one I mean—I'm not being that, because I don't just go around preaching some form of anarchy or, you know, that Wild West–type philosophy, "Might makes right." I don't. I'm a totally responsible citizen and am not into all that, so you know that I'm telling you the truth when I say that you are the injured party here. She left you. Correct? All the circumstances in the world don't mean anything—she *left*. So . . . you do it, you go get back what is yours and you're gonna sleep a lot better tonight. The kids, I mean, you can't deal with that now, you can't, that's a matter for the courts and all, our *legal* system, but there's nothing written or unwritten that says someone can take up ownership of your Nintendo 64 just because they want to. I mean, so what? I want a bunch of stuff—I feel the need for a new phone or one of those little Palm Pilot jobbies, doesn't mean I can just march down to Circuit City and take 'em off the shelves. (*Beat.*) I'm just a guy who stands up for what's right. I mean, what *I* figure is right, whether it is or not. 'Cause that's all you can do, is look at a thing, something that happens or takes place, and then decide. Make your decision on how you feel about it and then take a stand.

The MAN *ponders this for a moment, checks his mirrors, then goes back to talking. The* OTHER MAN *stares off.*

MAN It's like the other night—maybe two, three nights ago—I go to the movies, off to the cinema to see this film. An action film, but also filled with serious parts, too. One of those kind. With that one guy. And as it's about to start, in fact, has started, we're a couple minutes into the thing, the projector begins acting up. It's, like, sliding all these different lens thingies in the way, rotating them into frame and screwing up the picture. It even burned out for a second, you know the way you used to see it, where the image sort of melts up there in front of you? It did that. Right on this lady's face, as she's smiling at the hero guy, that one guy, who's holding a gun on her. *Training* it on her, and the film burns up. So I sit there in the dark for a bit, no more than a minute or two, eating my Twizzlers and stuff, and the thing comes back on, we watch the rest of the show. No problems. Point being—and I have one here, I'm not just running on to waste time while we're driving—I'm going into the bathroom afterward, past these two people at the candy counter who're talking to the salesgirl there. Some little redhead. So, I'm brushing past when the woman reaches out—not the girl, but the lady, the older one—she reaches for me and grabs my jacket and stops me, this look on her face. Some sour look, and says, "Can you please back us up here?" See, she's complaining about what happened . . . the picture thing . . . and wants her money back. Sat *through* the whole damn feature but is now asking for a credit. A free ticket for a later time, because of this little gaffe. And the guy next to her—I mean, they're not together, like a couple or anything, but they are linked in their "outrage" here—he adds to the mix, "It was intolerable!" I'm not kidding you, he used that word: "intolerable." And they look at me to validate this, to throw my hat into the ring with them, and I say, quite blandly, "Geez, you must be shit in a crisis." They look at me—I don't think it really registered completely, that I might be disagreeing with them— when I add, "If *that's* 'intolerable,' then you better run for cover, 'cause you're not gonna make it through life." And I meant it, too, you know? I mean, come on . . . a free pass because they missed a little chunk of some crap film that they both used the senior discount on? I hate that stuff, things like that. I really do. It bugs me . . . Anyhow, he was gay, not that it matters much, but he was. And they're like that sometimes. Gay people are. You know, *prissy* about things.

A bit more silence creeps in for a moment. The MAN *continues.*

MAN Anyhow, I simply offer that up as evidence of my impartiality in this matter. My absolute down-the-middleness in your getting your property back. I mean, she's acting like you want the *Xbox*, for chrissakes, all the noise she's making about it! Jesus, it's . . . they don't even make *games* for the damn thing anymore, you know? It's not about that. It's about principle and fair play and that type of consideration. If you just grab-and-run, if you do that, then hey, we're back in the Stone Ages. Or Africa, at least . . . which I guess is much the same thing, depending on which history books you read. (*Beat.*) Listen, point I'm making—I play fair, I do, even when it costs me a free trip back to the movies, so, you know . . . I don't say it 'cause we're buddies, or because I'm dying to play a little Mortal Kombat or whatever, I say it because it's true. *Truth.* That game console is yours, plain and simple. Now, you decide what you wanna do about it . . . (*Beat.*) I'm gonna just keep driving until you come to some finality on the issue.

The OTHER MAN *looks over at him, considering. Silence.*

OTHER MAN Go down Division.
MAN Now you're talking . . . now you are *talking*, my man! Oh yeah.

The MAN *executes a right turn and smiles as he does it. The* OTHER
MAN *stares out the window.*

MAN Oh my. Oh my, my, my, oh my. Yes, yes, yes! Time has come
today—like in that one song, you know . . . "Time has come
today!"—time, she has come and someone had better be ready,
you know? They-better-be-ready, 'cause the readiness is all. It is.
Somebody, and I'm not naming names, but some lady with a new
boyfriend and who's feeling no pain . . . she had better take
heed. That's all I've got to say, and I'll say no more. Someone
had better take some goddamn heed . . .

*They drive on, bopping their heads to an imaginary beat, both
looking straight ahead.*

road trip

A MAN *and a* GIRL *driving cross-country. She is asleep but slowly wakes up.*

MAN Hey.

GIRL Hi.

MAN How you feeling?

GIRL Okay.

MAN Just okay?

GIRL Yes. It was bumpy when I was sleeping. It seemed bumpy . . .

MAN There was construction.

GIRL Oh.

MAN Down to one lane in some places.

GIRL Hmm. Well, I'm fine. I guess . . .

MAN Sure?

GIRL Uh-huh. Still tired . . .

MAN Well, sure, of course you're tired. We've been driving a long time so it's easy to tire out.

GIRL How long?

MAN Most of today . . . since yesterday afternoon. When school got out.

GIRL Time is it now?

MAN Two-thirty. Almost. You'd still be in gym.

GIRL Huh.

MAN Yeah.

GIRL So, we've done, like, almost twenty-some hours? On the road, I mean.

MAN About that, anyway.

GIRL Wow.

MAN It goes fast, doesn't it?

GIRL Pretty fast.

MAN Well, not like a *rocket*, but still . . . fast enough. You slept for quite a while this morning.

road trip

GIRL I was sleepy.

MAN I know.

GIRL I tried to stay awake, but I was . . .

MAN It's okay. I know.

GIRL I . . .

MAN What?

GIRL Nothing.

MAN No, go ahead. Go on. You what?

GIRL I just . . . kinda miss my friends.

MAN I know you do. I know that. We talked about it, remember?

GIRL Yes.

MAN They're your friends, so you're going to miss them. That happens.

GIRL 'Kay.

MAN Any time you go away you miss your friends. Or family. That's just natural.

GIRL I guess.

MAN It's absolutely true.

GIRL Huh.

MAN I promise. Anybody in their right mind would miss their parents when they go off somewhere for a while. Camp, or traveling, or whatever. Boarding school.

GIRL Yep.

MAN My folks sent me to military school when I was seven. Seven years old and I was shipped out to this place in Virginia. Spent four years there.

GIRL Really?

MAN Oh yeah. Little uniform and everything.

GIRL Cool.

MAN I didn't think so, not one bit. Used to cry my eyes out like a toddler all the time, each night. Wanted my parents to come get me so badly. Didn't let the other guys catch me—crying, I mean. But I did it, all the same.

GIRL Sorry.

MAN Hey, that's . . . it's the past. Right? That's why they call it that, "the past," because that's what it is. Past.

GIRL Probably.

MAN They do. It's not just some made-up word, convenient for journalists or scholars or whatnot . . . It means what it is. It's the perfect word for it. "Past."

GIRL That's true.

MAN It is. It's very true.

GIRL Are you still mad at me?

MAN What?

GIRL Angry with me. For being so . . . you know. When we first got started.

MAN No, not at all.

GIRL Sure?

MAN I'm very sure.

GIRL Good.

MAN It's all right, I understand.

GIRL You do?

MAN Of course. You were scared. It's a big deal, driving across the country for the first time, obviously you're gonna be a little nervous.

GIRL I didn't mean to hit you.

MAN Doesn't hurt.

GIRL I'm glad . . .

MAN Stings a little, but . . .

GIRL Really?

MAN No, I'm joking with you.

GIRL Ahh. 'Kay . . .

MAN It's fine. No problems.

GIRL Great.

MAN Made me mad at the time, obviously, but . . .

GIRL Sorry.

MAN No, it's all right, I'm just saying . . .

GIRL What?

MAN Telling you the truth. I understand now, but it pissed me off when you were doing it. Hanging on to that bathroom door and kicking at me like you were . . .

GIRL I know.

MAN Really got me hot, and so that's why I yelled at you. Raised my voice like that.

GIRL All right.

MAN I'm not usually that way. You know that, right? I mean . . .

GIRL Yes.

MAN You know I'm not some loud person, ranting and raving and all that sort of nonsense. Come on . . .

GIRL I know that.

MAN Good. Because I'm not. That is not me.

GIRL No, I've never seen you like that. I mean, except yesterday.

MAN Which I just explained.

GIRL Right. Hey . . . you wouldn't really have hurt me, would you?

MAN What?

GIRL That's what you said, as we were . . .

MAN I know, but I was . . .

GIRL Anyhow, you said it and it made me all, I don't know. Frightened.

MAN I'm sorry.

GIRL You wouldn't, though, right? Do that . . .

MAN Do I seem like I would? Huh?

GIRL No, but . . .

MAN All right, then.

GIRL It's just that you seemed, I dunno . . . It was scary.

MAN Well, I'm an adult. Adults are scary. I mean, sometimes.

GIRL Okay.

MAN Your mom yells, doesn't she?

GIRL Yes.

MAN I know she does.

GIRL Yeah, she can shout pretty good.

MAN I've heard her. At school, even . . . in the halls, the times she's come to pick you up and screaming in your ear. I've seen her do it.

GIRL I know you have.

MAN So, fine. I'm just saying people do that sometimes, when they get frustrated or at the end of their rope. They holler. Say things they don't mean.

GIRL Right.

MAN You were acting like a baby out there, middle of nowhere, and it was hot and I lost my temper, that's all. I already said I was sorry.

GIRL Okay. Me too.

MAN But you can't act that way, I mean, not at a rest stop, people all over the place.

GIRL Sorry.

MAN It was embarrassing, and I just wanted to get going. Out of there. Families trying to have *picnics* under those little canopy things and you crying and carrying on like that. I just lost it . . .

GIRL I was mad.

MAN That's fine, I already said that. It's fine to show how you feel. Your emotions or like that. But not some big public display, that I can't stand.

GIRL Okay.

MAN I've told you that before—before this, anyway—and I meant it.

"Do whatever you want, but do it in private." That's a good thing to remember.

GIRL I will.

MAN Promise?

GIRL Yes.

MAN My father taught me that.

GIRL I know, you told me. And I will. Do that, I mean.

MAN Then good. Then I forgive you.

GIRL Thank you.

MAN Welcome.

GIRL Thanks.

MAN You know, you should've played soccer.

GIRL Huh?

MAN Soccer. You'd've been good at it, the kick you got there.

GIRL Oh. Yeah . . .

MAN I'm not kidding.

GIRL I know.

MAN Got a nice little way with your right foot.

GIRL You're just messing with me now.

MAN No, I'm totally serious. You do.

GIRL I never even made the team.

MAN You tried out?

GIRL Yep.

MAN When?

GIRL Last year.

MAN You tried out last season?

GIRL Uh-huh, I did. Got cut the last day.

MAN You never told me that.

GIRL Must've forgot. Anyhow, didn't get on the team, so it doesn't matter.

MAN Yeah, well, freshmen don't usually make the squad, anyway. So that's . . . It's good that you tried out. Good for you.

GIRL Thanks.

MAN I mean that.

GIRL Thank you.

MAN Team sports are a good thing, I think. Generally speaking, I mean.

GIRL Right.

MAN Not all of them, but most. Sometimes they get a little too serious, the coaches, some of the parents and like that, then it's not fun anymore. That's what I felt, anyway, when I was your age.

GIRL I play softball in the summers.

MAN I know that.

GIRL Oh, right. Yeah.

MAN I've watched you play.

GIRL That's right.

MAN And I'm just saying . . . good that you tried out for the soccer thing there, because it's a new sport and all that, just starting to take off in this country, and it's great to be a part of something new. That makes it special.

GIRL I don't really like it that much. Soccer.

MAN Well, they do everywhere else in the world.

GIRL I know.

MAN World's favorite sport.

GIRL Really?

MAN I think so . . . think I read that somewhere.

GIRL Wow. That's neat.

MAN Yeah. It's a big deal, most parts of the earth. In fact, they call it football, any other country does.

GIRL Really?

MAN Yes. It's their form of football, which makes sense, when you think about it.

GIRL It does?

MAN Sure. Look how much they use their feet when they play.

Kicking that thing all over the place. And in American football, we
hardly ever kick it.

GIRL For field goals . . .

MAN Yeah, and punts and kickoffs, I know. But I'm saying, overall. If
you watch a whole game, it's a pretty small part of what's
happening out there.

GIRL That's true.

MAN Look . . . over there . . . did you see that?

GIRL What?

MAN A deer. Two of them.

GIRL No . . .

MAN A mother and fawn. Just standing in the open.

GIRL I missed it.

MAN They were right there. In the brush.

GIRL Can we go back?

MAN No.

GIRL Please?

MAN No. Can't do that, but I'll keep my eyes out.

GIRL It's just right back over the . . .

MAN I said no.

GIRL Fine.

MAN Look out your window, you might spot one. Probably quite a few
around here, what with the terrain and all.

GIRL Yeah.

MAN Anyway . . .

GIRL . . . yep. Anyway . . .

MAN You hungry?

GIRL No.

MAN I've never known you not to be hungry.

GIRL Well, maybe. A little.

MAN That sounds more like it.

GIRL Just for a McDonald's or something.

MAN I'll stop if I see one.

GIRL 'Kay.

MAN Drive-through. Not inside.

GIRL Fine.

MAN Just because, you know. And it slows us down.

GIRL I just want a burger or something. Filet-O-Fish.

MAN No nutrition in those.

GIRL What?

MAN The fishwich.

GIRL That's not the name of it.

MAN Whatever they call it.

GIRL I just said. "Filet-O-Fish."

MAN Well, that one. The fish sandwich. You know what I mean, whether I've got the name right or not.

GIRL I know, I was just being funny.

MAN Hmmmm.

GIRL Silly.

MAN Well, it doesn't, no matter what you call it.

GIRL It doesn't what?

MAN It's not good for you.

GIRL I thought fish was a health-type food. You've said that before.

MAN That's the point. Fish is, but not the McDonald's fish. There's not much *fish* in it, I guess. Or it's the wrong kind.

GIRL Wrong kind?

MAN Of fish. Or not . . . could be shark.

GIRL Really?

MAN Sure. Companies do that . . . say you're eating one thing and actually dishing you up something else. Might be a hammerhead, or tiger shark, or some other sort of sea beast.

GIRL Eeeewwhh!

MAN Uh-huh.

GIRL That's nasty.

road trip   **77**

MAN I know it is. But it happens.

GIRL Well, I'm gonna just have a cheeseburger, then.

MAN Good choice.

GIRL And a Coke.

MAN Fries?

GIRL Okay.

MAN Then it's the meal.

GIRL Yeah, but not a big size.

MAN Just a plain meal. Fine.

GIRL Yes.

MAN Same for me. Quarter Pounder, though. I like the bigger onion pieces that they put on there.

GIRL They're different than the other ones?

MAN Oh yeah. They're, like, chopped for the regular sandwiches, little fine bits of onion, but on your Quarter Pounder, it's nothing but nice big chunks.

GIRL I never knew that.

MAN It's true. Take a look.

GIRL I will.

MAN Good.

GIRL My mom only lets me get regular cheeseburgers. They're cheaper.

MAN Huh. Well, with me, you can get anything you want.

GIRL Great.

MAN Except fish.

GIRL Okay. How long before we get there?

MAN Where, McDonald's?

GIRL No . . . where we're going. To this place. The cabin.

MAN You're excited about that, huh? Getting there, I mean . . .

GIRL Yeah. It sounds fun.

MAN It is fun.

GIRL Nice.

MAN And it's our little thing. A secret. Nobody knows about it, just you and me.

GIRL I like that.

MAN Me too. We can just relax and play house and do whatever you want to. Anything at all.

GIRL Go hiking?

MAN Of course.

GIRL And swim?

MAN Definitely. You can absolutely swim. Don't even have to wear a suit, I mean, if you don't want to.

GIRL I would. That's gross.

MAN Hey, it's not so bad. I used to do it when I was your age. When my family first started going up there.

GIRL Well, it sounds weird. That's skinny-dipping.

MAN No, it's nice. At least when it's nighttime . . .

GIRL Hmm. Maybe. I'd still be nervous . . .

MAN Yeah, but there's no one around there. It's very secluded, this place. Tucked away.

GIRL What's that mean?

MAN What?

GIRL "Secluded"? What do you mean by that?

MAN Hidden. Off the beaten track.

GIRL Oh. So, there's no other people around? Kids, I mean.

MAN Nope.

GIRL A phone?

MAN Uh-uh.

GIRL TV, though.

MAN Of course. Of course there's that. But no cable.

GIRL Huh. Okay.

MAN Just you and me. Like we said.

GIRL Yep. I got my Game Boy, anyway.

MAN Fine.

road trip

GIRL All right. How much farther? In miles . . .

MAN Umm, I don't know.

GIRL You don't know the way there?

MAN Yes, of course I do. I know how to get there, I just don't know
how long it'll take exactly. Number of hours or anything like that.

GIRL Well, just guess.

MAN No.

GIRL Come on, please . . .

MAN I don't wanna upset you if I'm wrong. If I say a figure, then
you're just gonna watch the clock and hold me to it.

GIRL No, I won't.

MAN Yes.

GIRL I won't, I promise.

MAN Sure?

GIRL Uh-huh. Very sure. Go on.

MAN Ummm . . . well, maybe most of today. A few more hours or
something. Around there.

GIRL Neat.

MAN About that, anyway. Roughly.

GIRL That's not so bad.

MAN No, I told you it wouldn't be . . .

GIRL Less than what we've done already . . .

MAN Exactly. Way less. And that's going the speed limit.

GIRL Which we should do . . .

MAN Which we *are* doing. Following the rules . . . same stuff I taught
you in Driver's Ed.

GIRL Yep.

MAN Always want to fit in.

GIRL Always?

MAN Most times. Yes. No need to stand out, make a scene. Leave
that for other people, outgoing-type people.

GIRL I'm outgoing.

MAN Yes, but not like that. Not all show-offy and everything.

GIRL No, I'm not. Not like those girls in pep squad or that kind of thing. Cheerleaders . . .

MAN Right, no, I hate that. That "look at me!" sort of girl.

GIRL I'm not that way.

MAN I know you're not. I know. And I like how you are.

GIRL You do?

MAN Very much. You know that.

GIRL Yeah, I guess.

MAN I've told you I do.

GIRL That's true.

MAN All right then . . .

GIRL Hey, there's a Burger King coming up.

MAN You want that instead?

GIRL I like McDonald's better.

MAN All right. Should we wait?

GIRL Yeah, let's.

MAN Fine. Then we'll just keep going. Going till we get there . . .

GIRL Okay.

MAN I'll keep an eye out for us. For those golden arches.

GIRL Maybe I'll rest some, then. Just until we pass one.

MAN You do that.

GIRL I'll take a nap.

MAN Yes.

GIRL Wake me when we . . .

MAN I will. Hey, can I touch your hair . . . just as we're driving, I mean?

GIRL Why?

MAN 'Cause it's relaxing. You're tired and it'll help you drift off . . .

GIRL Really?

MAN Sure. It's a kind of massage, is all. People do it to babies all the time. I'm sure your mom did it to you . . .

GIRL I doubt it.

MAN No, I bet she did, maybe when you were little.

GIRL . . . huh. Maybe.

MAN Anyhow. You want me to? It feels nice . . .

GIRL I guess . . .

MAN Is that all right?

GIRL Yeah.

MAN All right. Just a finger, even. Just my two fingers here in your hair, touching it . . .

GIRL Suppose so. If you want to . . .

MAN I do.

GIRL Why?

MAN I just do.

GIRL Fine. Doubt I'll sleep, though . . .

MAN That's no problem. I still want to. I want to do it.

GIRL All right.

MAN I do.

GIRL . . . 'Kay.

The GIRL*'s eyes flutter and close as the* MAN *continues to drive. He fingers her hair.*

autobahn

A MAN *and a* WOMAN *in the front seat of a car—the* MAN *at the wheel, the* WOMAN *on the passenger side. After a while, she speaks.*

WOMAN We just keep doing lousy things, I guess. That's what it is. All this lousy stuff that seems to finally catch up with us. Right? I dunno . . . it's hard not to feel that sometimes, this sense of, you know, regret. Well, maybe not that, maybe not real regret, like we were these Nazi war guards or whatever, hiding out in Nova Scotia and hoping that nobody figured out it was us when they show one of those films on the History Channel . . . but you see what I'm saying, don't you? 'Course. I'm sure you feel it, too. I think it's just the way it is these days, the whole country is living with this now, a kind of . . . well, whatever it is. A sickness. Yeah, a sick sort of feeling in your gut that says, "Hey, hello there, what's going on? I got a real ache in here that tells me we're up to no good." Now, that's just me being sort of dramatic about it, but it's like that. A still, small voice of some kind. (*Beat.*) I took Drama back in school, did I ever mention that? Oh yes. I was quite the little actress . . . had the lead in several productions and even sang a bit. Not much of a dancer—I've always thought that was a difficult art, don't you? Dancing—but I was known to carry a tune and could shed a tear on cue. Almost literally, on cue. That's what they call it in acting . . . your cue. When it's your turn to do something, and I was able, whether by gift or just practice, I could laugh or cry with the best of 'em. The best of Teddy Roosevelt Junior High, anyway . . . So, that's why I was doing that . . . acting out that bit just now.

They travel on for a while longer in silence. The WOMAN *glances over at the* MAN.

WOMAN Not that I think what we've done is so awful, I mean, on paper. Down on paper you see that people do this type of thing

autobahn

all the time . . . do it and go on quite happily with their lives. Absolutely true. (*Beat.*) It is "we," right? You felt the same way about things, I know you did, we talked it through and I think this was a very sensible decision on our part. Almost a sacrifice, really, when you think about it, because for the first few months it seemed like we were all very happy. It felt that way to me, anyhow. As if we were a family and were going to be that way for the rest of our days. Just like you'd see on any channel of the TV. Like on those half-hour comedy shows that they have out now. It felt just like that. But you never know, do you? No, you just never know what is going on inside the heart of a person, you can't really ever be sure. I mean, you look at them, study them at the counter or in the breakfast nook before they head off to school in the morning, but you can't really tell. (*remembering*) The first time he smiled at us, on that visit to the agency, do you remember that? I know he was sick, his nose all runny and everything, but it was like baby Jesus beaming up at you . . . that's what it seemed like to me. Like I was staring down into the manger or something . . . just brought him this big carton of that stuff they were carrying, the Wise Men—frankincense, I believe— and there he is, looking up at me with his big blue eyes and letting me know that this is the start of a glorious time. That's what it felt like to me. Now, I know, I know he was older than that, a baby, but I'm saying what it felt like. That was the feeling I got. And anyway, there aren't any pictures around of the teenage Jesus, so that's all I have to go on. The baby. Well, plus, the older ones, of course. The mature Christ. But he was, wasn't he? He was something almost nearly like that, like the Child himself . . . he was beautiful. Yes. (*Beat.*) I wonder if Christ really did have the blue eyes . . . you know, like they depict him on those shows? Hmm . . . I wonder.

She glances at her companion, then continues. He stares off.

WOMAN I know it's hard, I know that. It is completely hard and I can already feel the void that's there for me . . . for us. Plus the money. I'm absolutely aware of that part of it as well. But I don't think I could've taken another call from his counselor or the police, you know? I really don't think I could. When people start to look at you in the store—and I don't care if it's just Target or not—then it's time to do something. To step up and do what it takes to feel right and safe and like a good citizen. Don't you think? Well, I do. (*Beat.*) Plus, this car is not made for racing, isn't that what you said? I heard you screaming that at him last time, and I agree. This is not some high-performance vehicle that a person can just run up and down the access road like it was one of those deals they've got in Germany. What's it called, with the open, oh, come on, you know . . . the open speed limit? (*considers*) "Autobahn." That's it, an autobahn. Now, I don't know what that means, exactly, what it would translate to be in normal English, but we are not living near one of those, nor is he old enough to be out doing that. Taking the car out of the garage—I mean, why don't we just call it what it is, it's stealing, right? Plain and simple—and off joyriding around town. I don't care if he saw it in the movies or his friends put him up to it, which I don't doubt—that older Freeman boy is just an absolute terror—but he can't do that. He had many chances to stop, we gave him, well . . . nothing but chances, and he just couldn't stop. Couldn't stop going in my purse or calling us names or any of it, for that matter, not in the end. Could he? No . . . it was just too much. Too, too much, and that is not what we signed up for as foster parents. I'm no policewoman. I am not Angie Dickinson with a cute haircut and a gun in my bag. I'm a working adult and I

don't have time to do that. Be someone's mom. No, I don't
mean that, I was his mom, I am, but he just . . . you know
what it is? He was a pusher. He pushed us. Us, and the
limits, and anything else he could butt up against. Who knows
what his birth parents were like—I have an idea, thank you
very much—but he was someone who would just keep on
pushing until there was no room . . . left in the room. I know
that seems wrong, using "room" twice like that in a sentence,
but it's what it was like. You know what I'm saying. He left
you no space. No room in which to maneuver. (*Beat.*) Plus the
gun. I mean, my God! Taking a handgun to school, even if it's
just to show off to your classmates . . . that's the end. The
complete end, and that is that. Even the agency people told
us that. I don't know if you heard her, that redheaded one who
was in the back office, but she said we did the right thing.
She said—if you'll permit me the performance once again—
"You two have done the right thing here. Absolutely the right
thing." Looked me dead in the eye as she was issuing our
final check and said that, so I felt much better when I heard
it. I mean, I felt it, could feel it in my heart, but it's always
nice to have it validated. Your instincts. (*Beat.*) And we can
always bring someone else into our home, that's what they told
me. We're a level three on the clearance chart, so we're already
set up to do it again, if that's what we want. Maybe a girl this
time . . . wouldn't that be nice? And younger, maybe. That way, if
she was a bit younger . . . we could make a greater impression
right up front and then we wouldn't find ourselves in a spot like
this.

She looks over for some confirmation, but the MAN *continues to
stare out the windshield.*

WOMAN She also said, the redhead did, that this is completely
typical. The allegations that he's making. It's a common trick that
kids of his type do when they're brought back or have to be
placed in some other surroundings . . . it's quite usual for them
to say that they've been abused in some way. Sexually, or what
have you. I think it's sick and I'm very sorry that you've got to go
through this, honey, but she assured me that it happens all the
time and that nine times out of ten—actually she said eight,
eight times out of ten, but that's a very high number, too—it'll
often blow over. Charges dropped, or the kid will say it didn't
really happen or that kind of deal. So, no worries. And you know
that I believe you, right? You have my complete and utter support
. . . I mean, why would you ever lay a finger on the boy? Some
young boy whom we've taken in as our child, our son? I'm aware
that people do that, I'm not some naïve housewife who only
watches soaps and cooks pot roast, that is not me . . . I read
the paper and see the news and I know it happens, of course it
happens, but please. How could he do that? Tell the officer that
"things" of that nature had transpired? It just frightens me, it
really does. That he could have been under our roof, eating off of
our dinnerware, and been harboring a soul like that one. You just
never know, do you? No. Never . . .

The MAN *looks over at the* WOMAN *for a moment—he only looks away
when she looks back at him. She places a soothing hand on his
knee.*

WOMAN Well, it doesn't matter . . . it'll go away and then we'll be
right back where we were. All fine and good. Fine and good,
because we are that ourselves . . . fine and good people who
enjoy a place in the community. We reached out to someone, a

young someone who needed us, and I have no shame in that. I feel nothing but pride and want to do it again. Do you? Sweetheart? Don't you sense that we should do it again and let everyone know that this boy was a blip on the radar, a kind of, some sort of bad apple in the barrel, and we are not the problem. I do. That is exactly how this incident makes me feel and I have always been one to just jump back on the horse and ride. You know I am. (*laughs*) I even played Joan of Arc once, yes, I did, in a school play. Back in my class like I was telling you about. It's true. I carried this big papier-mâché horse around my shoulders on straps and had this cardboard armor on—I even had my mother cut all my hair shorter, that's how excited I was—and we told the story of that young French girl who became a hero and martyr for her people. I have a photo of it someplace, a snapshot that my uncle took of me . . . he was always taking pictures of me. My mother's brother. (*Beat.*) Anyhow, that is what we need to do. We have to get back on up and ride.

The MAN *nods without looking. The* WOMAN *picks up on this and smiles, happy to have some reaction from him.*

WOMAN That's the spirit . . . I realize that you were fond of him. Tried to make a life for that child and give him things. Show him how it all worked, being a man. And I in no way hold the gun thing over you, either. Feel that it was your fault for having that pistol in the house—we've already talked about that. It's a very good thing, it just might protect us one day. I agree. So, no. I think we were both . . . selfless and caring and perfectly in the right to do what we did. Some time back in a boys' home is exactly what he needs right now. Is crying out for, really. He was.

Was screaming it out and we just couldn't even see the signs. That's how much we loved him. Loved having him with us. (*laughs*) Maybe if he hadn't been crying it out at eighty miles an hour in our Cabriolet, we might've heard him a little better! Right? I think so. (*Beat.*) It's funny that . . . I read in a magazine somewhere, one of the many magazines I have—I know, I know, too many—I saw a breakdown of our lives, one of those pie-shaped thingies that takes time and divides it up into sections, and it said that we as a people spend about an eighth of our lives in cars. Yes. In automobiles. Isn't that remarkable? In our own cars, or the cars of others. Loved ones, mostly. Hmmm . . . maybe that's what he was doing, do you think? Driving like a madman around town because he loved us so much . . . maybe so. (*grins*) Oh well. It was quite interesting, anyway, when I read it. That article . . .

They drive on in silence, both looking straight ahead.

WOMAN And at least none of this has touched us. Right? I mean, the core of that thing which is us. What we have. That's what I'm most thankful for. That you and I . . . our union is not sullied by the experience. (*She considers.*) Am I using that word correctly? "Sullied"? I believe so . . . we remain untouched by this nonsense. Without sin, really. And that, in itself, is a blessing. I do have some sense of having done a bad thing, this kind of emotion that I mentioned before. I'm not sure why. The "lousiness" I spoke of, but I'm sure that will pass. I'm sure. It just comes with the territory . . . that woman, the one with the red hair, she said that as well. "This sort of thing comes with the territory." So that's a comfort. But the fact that it has in no way chipped away at our, you know—and I'm aware that you think I overdo the word "love," I know that, but—I'm just very happy that it hasn't.

She reaches over and touches him on the leg. Rubs it a bit. Finally, he glances over, touches his hand to hers, then removes it. Goes back to looking out.

WOMAN Yes, I know . . . I love you, too. I do, I do. Like Shakespeare said, "I love thee." Him or someone like him wrote that, anyway. I do love thee. (*Beat.*) I don't know, I just don't know . . . I'm sure he'll be . . . fine. At least for the night. He's been there before, God help 'im. He certainly knows the routine of that place . . . and tomorrow we'll call our lawyer, check in with ol' Mr. Thompson and put an end to all this other garbage in a heartbeat. One single heartbeat and a forty-cent call . . . Indeed, we will.

She studies the road now as he adjusts his mirror. There is quiet between them.

WOMAN Maybe the Germans have it right, after all. Not about . . . I don't mean in all ways, no, of course not. I certainly don't agree with their, you know, politics . . . but the car thing, that autobahn they've got there, maybe that's not a bad idea, actually. Perhaps that's the way it should be . . . all of us speeding by one another, too quick to stop, too fast to care . . . just racing along, off on our little journeys and no sense of how dangerous or careless we're being. Because we'd be safe, wouldn't we? Of course we would. Safe inside our bubbles of glass and steel—I suppose it's mostly plastic now, but you know what I mean— we'd be sheltered there, in these cars, as we moved along. All protected and careening about. Yes. And maybe then we wouldn't hurt so much. Or feel so deeply when we've been betrayed or hurt or lost. Yes. Yes, that might be just the thing. The very thing we need. (*Beat.*) And to think . . . it was right there in Germany, all these years . . . and we never saw it before this. No, we didn't. Not even once.

The WOMAN *glances at the* MAN *again, but he continues to stare out into the night. She returns to watching the road.*